Love's Twilight

by

Moody Holiday

Pretty Paper Press, LLC
New Jersey, USA

Love's Twilight
By Moody Holiday
www.moodyholiday.com

First Printing-November, 2003
Book Design Layout: Sisters' Computer Services
Sunset/Beach image: Copyright Superstock
ISBN: 0-9746315-0-7

This is a work of fiction. Any resemblance to actual people, establishments, places, locales and events are used fictitiously and is coincidental. References to historical figures reflect the time of the story. No historical figure whose name appears in this work has approved or otherwise participated in the creation of this work or endorses any of its contents.

The MHoliday design is a trademark of the author.

Printed In The U.S.A.

To all my well wishers
out there, I thank you.
Catrina, Kathy, Maalika, Rhodena, Tammy, Sally
Shawanna, Joy, Tommy,
Wendy, Beth, Gene and Joe

The Trilogy:

Wild Innocence, a Tale from the Eighties

Sweet Redemption

Love's Twilight

Love's Twilight

I searched the sky before twilight,
at times to no avail.
In an ocean breeze,
a bullet's wrath,
pierced a bittersweet fairy tale.

Thoughts of you seeped through me
like the sand in an hourglass.
It settled on auburn leaves
and surrendered among the grass.

Nothing among this earth can
replace your everlasting love.
I caress your sweet redemption
as you gaze from heaven above.

Whisper to me Alex,
before twilight,
I await your call.
I see you among the horizon,
as summer anguishes into fall.

Hope rises with the dawn,
life moves along,
two feet planted strong.

Fate spirals into destiny
With him is where I belong...

Table of Contents

If I Only Knew

The under cover federal sting operation called "Sitting Bull," shut down too soon. Now that I look back on all the things that happened to me, instead of closing up shop, the feds should have obtained a warrant to wiretap Rico's phone calls in prison. If they did, maybe Alex would be alive today.

Wiretapping, photographing and surveillance ended on the day of the bust. Federal agents from the joint narcotics and weapons units closed up shop with a firm handshake as black Chevy Caprices drove out of the Garvey Projects. Confident in their drugs and weapons seizure, they made their presence known by driving down the pothole riddled street in a slow, parade like procession.

Scorned residents followed closely behind and flashed them the middle finger. They were happy to have less crime in their neighborhood, but furious that two staples in the community were headed to federal prison.

Life at Garvey was a double edge sword. Mama Barb, the fearless cook for the entire apartment complex and the second lead suspect, was hauled out of her apartment with tight plastic cuffs piercing into her chubby wrists. Back inside, federal agents made a mockery of her two-bedroom flat as they kicked, flipped and showed off items that had nothing to do with their investigation.

"What the hell is this?" one agent asked, as he held up a cold jar of fresh hog mogs soaking in cloudy vinegar. The sight of pig skin and flesh caused his face to scour up in disgust.

"Damn," he replied, "We may have to call in the Haz Mat unit for this shit."

A senior narcotic agent laughed and said, "Quit playing Dobson, we're looking for controlled substances. Make sure you check the ice cube trays too, if they're empty, let them sit out so we can swab the interior for residue."

Shattered glass stuck to the senior agent's feet as he dragged the soles of his shoes across Mama Barb's bedroom floor for one last photograph. Evidence of her morning routine caught the agent's attention as his eyes shifted to a small light flickering on her Rowenta iron. Mama Barb usually took a shower after her chicken dinners were packed. Her freshly ironed clothes would never be worn again as they laid to rest on her cherished maple trunk at the foot of the bed. She never had a chance to dress herself. The agents squashed what little dignity she had by forcing her out of the apartment in a soiled housecoat riddled with grease stains. Not one rat-tooth comb in her reach graced her appearance to smooth out the back of her thinning hair. Mama Barb's auburn highlights stood straight up like a rooster under the still of morning twilight. Her moist slippers did little to compliment her style or gait as she hobbled down the walkway to a government vehicle.

Anxious members of the press stood by with their feet planted firmly to the ground. They had a field day at her expense, as flashing light bulbs forced her eyes into a startled reaction.

Children of various ages stood at the fence crying

as urban history took place. Mama Barb was a staple of love and consistency as news of arresting agents entering the building spread through the complex like wild fire.

The weak, weary and the nosey, jumped out of bed, hobbled to window sills or ran downstairs in tee shirts, doo rags and house slippers to see the commotion. The child that stood out the most along the horizontal fence was little Corinthia. Mama Barb rocked that girl in the comfort of her bosom and on her hip for the first two years of her life, while her mother hit the streets looking for a hustle and a hit. The sassiness in her two-year old voice won Mama Barb over every time she came to her door with a bag of chips and a quarter juice in her hands. Corinthia had butter brown skin, thick eyebrows and piercing green eyes. Silver caps gripped every tooth in her mouth, so Mama Barb did everything in her power to keep her away from sugar.

Corinthia gripped her petite two-year old fingers through the iron fence and wailed in shivering agony as if it were her own mother. In her short time on earth, this was Corinthia's second psychological abandonment. The older kids held on to Corinthia's shoulders just to keep her from jumping over the fence and into Mama Barb's arm.

Mama Barb turned her head around to give one last instruction before she got in the car. She forced her head back up and shouted, "Kia! Take Corinthia to Ms. Jenkin's house until her mother gets home and don't give her any candy!"

Because of Mama Barb, many children escaped the wrath of Child Protective Services just by living near and dear to her heart. No matter how kind, the motherly love she provided ended on the day of the bust.

A small tear rolled down Mama Barb's deep-set eyes and over her high cheekbones. She knew she wasn't coming back and she was thankful her son Mookie was at basketball practice instead of seeing his dear mother dragged off by the arm of the law.

As for Rico, he went out in grand style with shackles on his wrists and legs escorted by four buffed federal agents. He looked good no matter the time or trouble. Rico pimped out of the quad with a cocky ass grin on his flawless face. He even flexed his muscles to enhance his "Enter the Dragon" tattoo on his bicep. Residents shouted from their apartment windows in various temperaments and languages.

"Keep yo' head up nigga!" One of his boys said, as he pulled his handkerchief down past his mouth, quickly pulling it back up again.

"We love you Rico," said one of his many adoring girlfriends. Tamika looked up to see what window it came from. She was pissed off when she saw him leave. He tipped heavy even if it was a five-minute blowjob. Seeing Rico leave was a financial hardship for her because she didn't have to go far to turn a trick. On any giving day, she never missed her favorite soap opera as long as Rico was in the complex.

As the feds made their final exit, small pieces of revenge and anger were hurled at them. They were cursed at, spat upon and a few elder residents threw vexes on them by throwing old chicken bones at their feet. The feds didn't care what the residents did as they walked out with smooth grins on their faces. In their minds, the people of Garvey were just a bunch of "shitums," as they called them.

That night, the feds celebrated at Krug's Pub on Ferry Street. It was the same night Alex came home in a drunken tirade when I was pregnant with Troy. He participated on the evidence inventory team when the bust was completed. Captain Fisco waited for things to cool down before he convinced the feds to let Alex take part in the clean up operation. In retrospect, that was the reason why Alex was so pissed off about Nikki coming to the house when Troy was born. If the feds or Captain Fisco heard about Nikki's visit, Alex would have been in big trouble.

Jack was also at Krug's Pub for the grand cigar and cigarette filled celebration. They sat around in black boots and fatigues to toast their success, while I laid in bed wondering where my husband was. It took a while for me to put the pieces together. The New York Times was the only paper that provided a succinct time line of events. I should have been trying to figure this stuff out before Alex was gunned down, but I didn't have a reason to be suspicious.

My life and life at the Garvey Street Projects would never be the same. Nobody reaped any immediate benefits out of the bust except for the local cops and feds. They dipped, sampled and split up their cut without blinking twice. They had a solid case against Rico and Mama Barb. That was all they needed to shut their operation down for good.

Payback

The swell and temperament in the projects settled in three days after Rico got a message back to his crew that he was treated kindly and eating well. A few loyalists threw a pity party just to help Rico with his legal fees. Three hundred and thirty three dollars didn't put a dent in his bill, but he appreciated the urban act of kindness.

Rico sat in jail cool and collected despite his sixteen count federal indictment. After a momentary pause, he spit in the corner of the hallway, slicked his curly damp hair back with his hands and picked up the pay phone.

"Yo Flaco, get in touch with my sister and tell her she owes me one. I need info on Foster. I could fuck with Nick, but I'm gonna need him for now, I know he still wants in. We need to send him a warning that he's still our bitch. In the mean time, I'll fuck up another good 'ole boy on the take."

Rico was pissed off that an eleven month operation got by him without any word from Nick. A payback was the only way Rico could put Nick on notice that his turn was next if he didn't cooperate in the future. He could have easily killed Nick, but he always had valuable information for Rico, including new spots in other parts of

North Orange that were open and accessible to drug trafficking. Rico definitely wanted revenge, but Nick was too valuable. Instead, Rico chose Alex.

Rico's cousin and underground flunky hung up the phone and called Nikki.

"No," Nikki said, "I don't see Shanelle too much, she just had a baby."

Nikki cleared her throat while she stroked Tammy's perky nipples. "Nah," she answered with little suspicion, "He threw me out of his house a few weeks ago because of the investigation."

Tammy rolled over and whispered, "Who's that?"

Nikki covered the phone and said, "Shh, it's my cousin."

The conversation ended just like that. Nikki quietly hung up the phone, rolled over on top of Tammy and slowly kissed her to silence any lingering curiosity. Flaco dropped the phone on the receiver and smiled with criminal intent in his eyes. He was ready for a promotion and he knew this job would do the trick.

Flaco was Rico's first cousin. He grew up in East Orange with his mother and younger sister. After one rape trial ended in a hung jury at the ripe old age of eighteen, Flaco fled to the Bronx until things settled down. He tried to make a name for himself out there, but he failed. When he went back home to his mother's house, she changed the locks and forbade him to return. His little sister revealed a dirty secret to their mother, which confirmed her suspicions about her son's seedy appetite. Desperate and no where else to go, Flaco sought refuge with Rico and he quickly put Flaco to work. His main job was quick stick ups and getting information passed on to Rico from the outside. On the day I went to Garvey to watch Mookie play basketball, an undercover street agent, wearing a wire, picked up Rico and Flaco's conversation right after

Rico told me to leave. No wonder the feds and Alex were so adamant about my safety. The conversation went down like this:

"Damn, who was that sweet piece of ass that just left, I swear I know her from somewhere?"

"That's Shanelle, Steven's little sister?"

"Word?"

A photograph from the seventh floor captured Rico pulling a drag from his cigarette before he dropped it to the ground.

"Yeah, but she's off limits, she's married to five-o, one of Nick's boys."

"Word?"

"Yeah, Magilla Gorilla, you've seen him before."

"Right, right, but I remember a nice piece of ass when I see one."

A second photograph captured Flaco snapping his fingers.

"Oh... now I remember, I tried to tap that ass one night in East Orange, but that nasty bitch threw up on me."

Rico could be heard saying, *"You proud of that you dirty mother fucker, you better not fuck with her!"*

It was enough dialogue to force the feds to take a closer look at me and figure out why Rico was so invested in a cop's wife. Strange as it sounds, Rico looked out for me in a small way by telling me to leave Garvey that day.

When we were younger, Rico walked me home from Metcalf Park in the Valley. When we got to Scotland Road, he asked me if I wanted an Italian Ice from Cocquelle's Bakery. He was too cute to resist, so on that quiet summer day we walked five long blocks to get there. He nervously pulled four crumpled dollar bills out of his pocket. He told me he was going to be rich. I believed him as I licked my desert and thanked him for my Italian Ice.

Once outside, he planted a cold kiss on my cheek before he walked me home. It was an innocent fifth grade kiss that meant more to him than to me. We rarely saw each other as years went by, but every time I ran into him, we shared an innocent smile of the childhood we left behind.

I think his innocent crush stayed with him even in his darkest days of deviancy, but it wasn't enough to keep Alex alive. Garvey was his family's lifeline and keeping it under his control while he remained in jail was his number one priority.

Alex was as vigilant as Rico was about controlling the world around him. He blamed the whole thing on Tammy after she left our house with Nikki. Alex told her on too many occasions, that when the real shit goes down, families stick together no matter the reason. Unfortunately, love and lust had Tammy so mixed up she was blind.

Nikki accepted Tammy's full frame and big hips. When she was with Nikki, it didn't matter what she ate. Tammy felt comfortable on the outside, whenever she hung out with Nikki, because Nikki didn't care about anything but herself and the girl by her side. The only time she paid attention was when Rico called. There was no way she could ever repay her mother and father for all the toilets they scrubbed to put her through St. Amelia's High School. Even though Rico earned money the illegal way, he made sure his sister didn't want for nothing at Pitt University. When Alex threw them out of the house after the baby was born, she thought it was funny and quickly forgot about it. It was all the ammunition Rico needed.

Rico went back to his cellblock confident. He knew four visits with his sister would get him the right information. Like clockwork, Nikki visited her brother four times over an eleven-month period. On every occasion, she had diarrhea of the mouth, especially when it came to Alex and I.

Two weeks before Candy's wedding, Rico put in a bid for a female shooter.

"Listen Flaco, let Gigi do the job, that bitch is good yo, she never misses. Make sure you saw off the handle and barrel for her. You got that Flaco?"

Flaco didn't answer, the dial tone in Rico's ear cemented their conspiracy.

One Week of Happiness

"*Happy birthday dear Troy...Happy birthday to you!*" The noise in our kitchen was enough to make the meekest child cry out in fear as friends and family sang happy birthday to our son. Troy balled up his fat fingers into two fists and blew out the candles like a champ. He clapped in unison as everyone cheered for him. At one year old, I wasn't surprised. I practiced with him for an entire week simply because I had so much time on my hands. Gone were the days of juggling classes and exams. Alex's constant need for me and tending to Troy's every whim took me away from my dreams. College took a back seat on the highest bookshelf in our house. Just talking about school stirred Alex in the worst way. He was so worried about the trial and the intrusive press coverage surrounding the Garvey Street bust, he found little time to relax. A fretful thirty pound weight loss had everyone buzzing about him. Some speculated that he was hitting a crack pipe, while I begged him to eat because he looked so thin. So much was going on in our lives, I decided to wait until after the trial to resume classes. He loved the idea and became a calmer man. His greatest joy was coming home to Troy and I every night. After a good home cooked meal and thirty minutes of his own time, he was truly the king of our modest castle. The domestic hustle and bustle did little to enhance my self worth. I felt like an old maid all the time and my girl Candy made a point of reminding me every time she saw me. Troy's first birthday was no exception.

"Shanelle," she said, after handing me the cake knife, "Go upstairs and take that raggedy ass sweatshirt off, you look like a bum."

Even though Candy whispered her message, it landed right in Alex's ears. He cut Candy a look as he passed out two slices of cake and then grabbed me by the arm.

"She looks good to me no matter what she wears." Alex kissed my forehead and winked at me with love in his eyes. When he let go, I looked down at my clothes and said, "You're right Candy, I should change."

Alex, of course, had other plans. "Shanelle, make my father a plate and wrap it up, he's ready to go."

I looked at Alex and then Candy before I responded.

"Uh, ok, I will."

Troy grabbed my leg as I walked into the kitchen.

"Mamee, Mamee, up!" he said, as he stretched his arms in the air. I scooped him up and kissed his chunky chin as he playfully smacked my cheeks. I quickly switched him to my other hip as the phone rang. Alex and I picked it up simultaneously as the intruder started his inquiry.

"Mrs. Foster, do you have any comments regarding your brother Steven's mysterious accident at Garvey?"

Alex's response was swift. "Hang up the phone Shanelle."

I quickly hung up the phone as Alex dealt with the call. With less than two weeks to go before the trial and

Candy's wedding, Alex was damn near going crazy with anger and suspicion. Candy was getting on his last nerves too, because she was a gossip pipeline from North Orange to Brick, New Jersey. Candy quickly came to my rescue and fixed a plate of food for Alex's father. While the Fosters bid us goodbye with hugs and kisses, Candy slapped some foil over his plate and threw it in a Shoprite bag. Once they were out the door, I winked at her and smiled as she followed me upstairs to Troy's room.

"Shanelle," Candy said, "Why don't you spend the night at my house so we can go to Mueller's in the morning?"

"What's at Mueller's?" I asked.

"I want to make some baskets for the bridal party," Candy said.

"Why?" I asked, "It's just me and Bonnie anyway."

"Don't worry about it Shanelle, can you come?"

Candy started taking Troy's birthday outfit off while I ran some water in the tub. He was sleepy, but he needed a good bath to get him to sleep comfortably through the night. After pouring some baby bath in the water, I picked up Troy and put him in the tub. He laughed and splashed the water so hard that Candy stood back to avoid getting wet.

"I don't think that's a good idea," I said. "Alex really likes me to be home and we just finished Troy's party." I handed him a yellow duck and said, "Hey, we'll get up at five o'clock and meet you in the morning, that way we'll have the whole day."

Troy let us know his father was coming just by the sound of his heavy footsteps.

"Daaadee! Daaadee!"

Alex's entrance into the bathroom immediately crowded our space as I stood between him and Candy. He smiled at me and threw a towel over his shoulder as

Candy stood sideways to step out. Candy followed me out and sucked her teeth at the sound of the bathroom door closing. What followed was an orchestra of grunting and laughing as Alex and Troy acted out father bear and baby bear. While we walked down the hall, Candy gave me a stern look and whispered, "That shit sounds ridiculous, but at least we can go to breakfast first."

Candy helped me straighten up Troy's room as we planned our day. She gave me a quick peck on the cheek and said, "Let me get out of here, Clinton has a flight in the morning. I'll get everyone out, you get a good night sleep. By the way, great party."

I rolled my eyes in my head while Candy playfully bid me farewell with a Miss America wave. Peering over the balcony, I could hear laughter from a distance as Candy teased the lingering guests downstairs.

"Black folks, y'all sure don't know when to go home." Then she laughed out loud and said, "Oh, I'm sorry Jack, you don't look it, but I swear you got some black in you too."

Warm steam escaped from the bathroom. Alex cracked the door and looked in my direction. Water seeped on the floor and splashed on Alex while he washed Troy's feet. I smiled as I listened to him try to make sense out of his baby babble.

"You did?" Alex asked, "And then what happened?"

Troy splashed the water again and held his head back in weary laughter. Alex stood up and lifted him out of the tub. Our son had so many shiny rolls on his skin, Alex had to separate the creases and wipe out the moisture so he wouldn't get a rash. After a puff of baby powder escaped from his pamper, Troy's eyes opened and closed in complete exhaustion. I exhaled quietly as I watched the two of them. My smile widened as Alex walked out the bathroom with Troy's head nestled on his shoulder. Alex turned on his night-light and put our baby giant in the crib. Then he put his arm around me as we watched Troy snuggle into his warm surroundings. The sound of his musical mobile forced me into a heavy yawn as Alex rubbed my shoulders. Even though we were in tune to our sleeping son, it didn't take long for Alex to start asking questions.

"What time are you coming home tomorrow?"

I took a deep breath and said, "One o'clock, Troy will probably sleep the whole ride home."

Alex followed me into the bedroom and put on a dry tee shirt. He didn't care that guests were shuffling out the door as he pulled me on top of him and then rolled over. He exhaled in my neck while I kissed the stress lines on his forehead. The relief of my soft affection settled his wrinkles. We stared into each other's eyes like any couple searching for serenity during times of happiness mixed with stress. All I could do was be there for him even though I began to doubt his conscience. Alex closed his eyes and began to think out loud.

"I love you Shanelle."

"I love you too," I replied.

My eyes met his and I searched for answers to his worry.

"Let me help you Alex, talk to me, tell me."

He immediately shook his head to negate my concern.

"There's nothing to tell Shanelle, don't worry, everything is going to be okay."

My lips quivered slightly with doubt. "You're getting so thin Alex, you don't feel like a teddy bear anymore."

He seemed surprised at first and then remembered his brawn and strength by looking at a picture of us on the beach last year. He stretched out his fingers and slowly pressed them into my back.

"You're right baby, I'm going to eat, I promise." Alex pinched my earlobe and said, "If anymore calls come in Shanelle, just let the machine answer." After that, he immediately lifted me up off of him and quietly went downstairs.

It was definitely my cue to get off his back about the ordeal we were going through. There were so many phone calls I couldn't keep up with the endless questions and requests for interviews. The press was frustrated with the case because nobody wanted to talk, especially the good citizens of Garvey. Steven's mysterious accident put everyone on notice to mind your damn business. The local cops made sure it stayed quiet by posting extra police officers in the day and evening. Candy kept clippings from the Essex Chronicle to keep me informed, but none of it seemed to matter because I was so far away. Meeting the girls the next day brought me right back into the action.

Bonnie met us at the Harris Diner for breakfast with all the dirt. "Look at fat boy Troy," she said, as she quickly grabbed him and tried to put him in a wooden high chair. His fat legs quickly resisted as he kicked the chair with his white Stride Rite walking shoes.

"He doesn't like high chairs," Candy said.

Bonnie could barely manage as she handed him back to me.

"Girl, what are you feeding him?"

Candy laughed and said, "Girl she just took him off the titty last week!"

Bonnie's eyes got wide and said, "Damn Shanelle, were you enjoying that too?"

The waitress passed out the menus as Troy bounced up and down on my lap.

"I'll pretend I didn't hear that you freak." I replied.

Bonnie smirked and said, "Speaking of freakin' at the Freaknik, what's up with Tammy and Nikki, I hear they're closer than close."

Candy busted out laughing, but I didn't find it funny.

"You don't even know them," I said, "So you need to mind your business."

Bonnie sipped some of her water as her eyes shifted between two conversations, "I love you too Shanelle. Don't get me wrong, I think Tammy is cool, but does Nikki know how to mind her own business?"

I put some bread in Troy's mouth to calm him down and asked, "Well, what do you mean by that?"

Bonnie's constant pursuit of hot news kept her connected to the underground gossip.

"Me and Andre saw Rico's cousin Flaco last week outside the Shelter. You know they lit up a spliff and started talkin' about this and that. Anyway, Flaco said that Nikki kicks it with your sister-in-law for free food and a bed at Pitt."

I didn't know who Flaco was at the time, so I asked out of sheer curiosity.

"Who's Flaco?" I asked.

"Oh," Bonnie said, "That's his punk ass cousin from East Orange." She paused a minute and said, "Yeah, I think he used to live on Fourth Avenue." Bonnie smirked and said, "He beat the rap on a rape charge, but Andre doesn't care because he said his weed is too, too nice."

I tried not to react, but I couldn't help it. I rolled my eyes up in my head, but I was getting pissed off.

"Yeah well, I'll talk to Tammy, but I can't pick and chose my sister-in-law's partners."

Candy was ready to hurl an assault as she looked down at her fork. I could see it coming just by the look in her eyes. She picked up her fork and said, "Yeah, whatever, I choose, capital DIC...," I quickly covered her mouth and said, "Candy chill!"

Bonnie started laughing as I fed Troy some pancakes.

Candy pushed my hand away and said, "Anyway, like I said, I prefer the pipe."

Bonnie started laughing and said, "Hold up, hold up, girl you free basing now?"

Candy looked at me and flashed a condescending smile while she pushed her plate away. Then she rolled her eyes at Bonnie and said, "Girl don't play with me, you know what I mean." She applied some pink gloss to her pouty lips and said, "Anyway, we're all set, right?"

Bonnie and I chimed in together and said, "Yes Candy."

"Good," she replied, "Dinner at Forno's Wednesday night."

"Forno's?" I replied, "You know I can't make that."

Candy slammed her compact mirror down and lifted her hands to the sky as Troy quickly mimicked his Godmother.

"Don't tell me, Alex right?"

Troy banged on the table as I bounced him on my knee to settle my own frustration. Before I could entertain her comment, Candy continued.

"Do me a favor Shanelle and take Alex to the next level."

I looked at her puzzled as Bonnie and I leaned in for one of Candy's profound statements.

"Alex is stressed the fuck out with all of this trial shit. He was riding your ass when I got to the party, during the party and after the party if my memory serves me correct. So do your marriage a favor, dim the lights, pour some wine, take a few sips and get on your knees girl."

Candy sat back in pure confidence as Bonnie

busted out laughing coupled with a high five.

"If you do that three times a week, Alex won't give a damn what you do." Candy said.

I rolled my eyes in my head as Candy nodded her head up and down.

"You can roll your eyes all you want, but you see how fast Clinton brings his ass home to me after a long flight. They don't call it a cock pit for nothing girl."

The laughter lasted longer as Troy started clapping at our girl talk. Candy pinched his cheek and said in a whiny high-pitched voice, "Even fat boy Troy knows what's up."

I got off the subject by concentrating on Bonnie. "So what are you doing for the rest of the week?"

"Nothing," Bonnie replied, "Just hanging out with Andre and getting cute for Candy's big day." She grabbed Troy's hand and said, "How is this Budda gonna make it down the aisle with his fat self? Are you going to bribe him with cookies?"

Candy sighed out loud and said, "He'll be okay, Alex is going to carry him if he gets cranky and his Auntie Tammy is coming for back up."

I smiled at Candy, happy that she was able to answer. I came up with the idea just so Alex and I could enjoy ourselves at the wedding. Tammy only saw Troy at Mrs. Foster's house after the argument she and Alex had when Troy was born. Honestly, I didn't think Alex was going to hold out that long, but he was determined to keep us safe from Nikki's crime family. Alex's good intentions meant little to the reality unraveling behind our back.

Rico's grand scheme fit right into my idea. He wanted "Gigi," to walk into the wedding disguised as Nikki and blow Alex away. In retrospect, Tammy fed her brother on a platter to Rico with her big fat mouth.

Bonnie looked at the two of us and smiled as she

rubbed Troy's hand. Candy picked up her glass of water and smiled at me as we shared a momentary lapse in conversation. If we only knew what was ahead of us, we would have called off the whole wedding and went into witness protection.

Candy threw her napkin down and motioned the waitress for the check.

"Let's go ladies, there's plenty of stuff to get done. I need your help picking out some dry flowers and that's it, so let's drive separate cars."

Bonnie looked at Candy and said, "This is the part where I get to say that you're starting to work my nerves Miss Bride to Be."

Bonnie's comment didn't phase Candy one bit as we walked out of the diner, so Bonnie put a small dent in the time table.

Candy got to Mueller's first and parked in the lot. As usual, Bonnie had to make a stop so we waited on the sidewalk for her at Central Avenue and Martin Luther King Boulevard. Troy stood between my legs as Candy looked for Bonnie's car.

"Where is that girl?" she asked.

"You know she likes to get lost, but she'll be here."

Cars were driving so fast I had to pay close attention to Troy as he tried to wander off. I barely had time to notice Candy's astute attention to a car slowing down in our direction. She tapped me on my shoulder and said, "Who's that waving at us?"

I picked up Troy as a white Toyota Camry pulled over. A light skinned woman with an attitude peered over her sun glasses as Derrick suddenly stepped out. He seemed relieved to get out the car because of his height. His big feet and green scrubs immediately gave him away as I looked up at him with Troy in my arms. Derrick was so fine he just took my breath away. He looked older and

more mature than ever. He cut his hair shorter and faded it
on the sides. I smiled when I looked at him in his scrubs
because I was proud that he stuck to his goals. I don't
think he would have settled for anything less.

"What's up Doctor Derrick?" Candy said.

A small smile caressed my face as I stared at Mr.
Handsome.

Derrick gave Candy a quick hug and immediately
focused on me.

"Shanelle, it's good to see you." He kissed me on
my cheeks and left his trademark cologne lingering on my
neck to enjoy a quick memory from the past.

Troy grabbed my sunglasses, put them in his
mouth and began to gnaw on the edges. I glanced at the
woman in the car first and then looked at Derrick. He
immediately stretched his hands out to hold my son and
said, "What's up little man?" Troy extended his left hand
out first as Derrick took him from my arms. He smiled at
Troy and said, "So, this was the big miracle holding your
stomach hostage?"

I smiled from ear to ear and quickly smoothed out
my clothes. "Yes, that's him."

It was strange looking at the two of them. Derrick
looked completely comfortable holding my son as the
woman in the Toyota beeped her horn and said defiantly,
"Rick, are you coming?"

Derrick hesitated at first and then said, "No, I'll get
a ride, call me later."

The window rolled up and she immediately sped
off towards downtown Newark. Her actions didn't faze
Derrick in the least as he tickled Troy's fat tummy and
immediately paid me a compliment.

"Wow Shanelle, he's healthy as a bull, what's his
name?" Troy patted Derrick's shoulders while Derrick
smiled at him."

In between my answer, smart ass Candy shrugged
her shoulders and motioned silently with her mouth,
"Rick?" She covered up her silly grin and laughed to
herself, as I answered Derrick's question.

"Ask him, he'll tell you."

Derrick immediately looked at Troy and said,
"What's your name?"

A mouthful of spit accompanied my son's answer
as he belted out, "Toy!"

I quickly corrected his pronunciation and said,
"His name is Troy."

My attention turned to the Toyota as I watched it
turn down University Avenue. Since it looked like he
wanted to see me for a little while, I decided to joke about
his new name.

"So tell me, who the heck is Rick?"

Derrick laughed out loud exposing his pearly white
teeth as he hoisted Troy in the air and said, "Can you say
Derrick?"

Troy mimicked him like a baby parrot.

"Deh dick!" Troy babbled.

"Wow," Derrick replied, "He's smart too."

"Thanks Rick," I replied.

Curiosity forced me to question his whereabouts.

"What happened to Cornell Med?"

"Nothing," Derrick replied, "I volunteer at
University Hospital whenever I come home. I'll be there
this summer too."

I took a deep breath and continued to stare at him.
I was happy to see him and curious at the same time. In
between his playtime with Troy, he continued to glance at
me and then quickly look away. Candy broke up the
moment and said, "Here comes Bonnie."

When Bonnie jumped out of the car, she quickly
apologized and sized up the scene.

"What's up Doctor Derrick?"

He gave her a quick peck on the cheek and said, "What's up? I see the three of you are still friends after all this time."

Bonnie replied, "We wouldn't have it any other way."

Derrick looked at his watch and said, "Ok, my ride left me, which one of you can take me to University?"

Candy took Troy from Derrick and said, "Shanelle of course."

I hesitated a bit and then looked at Candy as she winked at me. She snatched the diaper bag from my hand and said, "Make it quick."

I knew Troy was in good hands. He always went with Candy and this time was no different. I pointed to the Jeep Cherokee as Derrick put his arms around me and said, "It's so good to see you again Shanelle."

I smiled and said, "Thanks Derrick."

As we got in the car, I could feel his eyes all over me, especially my face. I looked at him and turned the ignition key as his fragrance began to light up the car.

"What?" I asked, as I began to smile.

"Nothing Shanelle, you look great. The last time we saw each other you were waddling like a duck remember?"

I turned at High Street and said, "Yes, I remember."

"I do have a confession," Derrick said.

"What's that?" I asked.

"I wanted that to last forever."

I looked straight ahead as cars pulled over at the New Jersey Institute of Technology. I slowed down a bit to take in what he said and replied, "As fat as I was…"

Derrick didn't let me finish. "You looked absolutely sexy pregnant, did anyone ever tell you that?"

I nodded my head and replied, "Yeah, my husband."

Derrick turned his head and stared out the passenger window replying, "Right... your husband."

I wasn't trying to rub it in his face, but it was an honest answer.

Derrick leaned back in his seat and asked, "Are you happy Shanelle?"

Funny, I was thinking the same thing, but he looked like he really needed to hear my answer. He began to stare at me again with such wonderment that I had to look straight ahead. In order to avoid the question, I pulled an Alex move and turned on the radio.

"So," I asked, "How many years left of school do you have?"

"This is it," Derrick replied. "I graduate next year and then my residency starts at University Hospital in July."

"So you're coming home?"

Derrick smiled and rubbed his face. "I have to Shanelle, you know I need to be with my community. There's a lot going on in pediatric AIDS research."

Derrick didn't forget his question. He simply rephrased it to me.

"I've been following the stories in the press Shanelle, I hope you're okay with all the exposure."

I looked at him with a blank stare. I didn't know where to begin or end as I avoided his inquiry. I stopped at a traffic light and asked, "Are you going to practice pediatrics?"

Derrick rubbed his chin with the tips of his fingers and shook his head. His answer was filled with confidence.

"Of course, I can't wait." Derrick watched the traffic as I responded to cars speeding by. He changed the subject and said, "I hope my patients are as healthy as Troy, you're doing a great job with him." He laughed and said, "Did you hear the way he said my name?"

I chuckled along with him and said, "Yeah, he's something else."

Our laughter faded into silence as I thought about Alex. I gave him some credit for my son's healthy disposition.

"We do a good job with him, especially his father." Derrick nodded his head in agreement and pointed in the direction of the hospital.

"Pull over here."

When I pulled over, Derrick turned the radio down and stared at me. My lips pressed together in nervousness, not knowing what he would do next. Derrick took my right hand off the steering wheel and held it in between his hands. I started to speak, but he silenced me with a kiss on my cheek.

"Don't say anything Shanelle, I'm leaving," he whispered.

I turned to say goodbye, but he began to shake his head like he didn't want to hear me say those words.

Derrick placed his lips to my ear and said, "Every time I see you, I swear I never want to let you go."

I looked down at my feet and bit my lip in sheer nervousness. He turned my head to look into his eyes and said, "Don't get me wrong Shanelle, I'm happy for you, but I regret letting you go even after all these years. With the trial coming up I hope you and your family will be safe."

I didn't utter a word. What could I possibly say to him after all this time? Derrick looked at me and said, "If you ever need me, you can look me up at University."

I cupped his face with my hands and said, "Thank you Derrick, I'll be fine."

Derrick grabbed my wrists and wrapped his fingers around the back of my hands. His thumbs pressed into my palms and forced my fingers to close. His energy was so calm that it forced me into a temporary trance. Derrick raised my left hand and opened it with a kiss. There was nothing I could say as I slowly pulled my hands away. The freedom in his eyes begged me to follow him but I couldn't. He took a deep breath and immediately got out the car. After he closed the door, he waved at me like he was never going to see me again. I flashed half a smile, and pulled off to meet Candy. If it wasn't for Troy, I would have stayed with him just because.

When I got back to Muellers, Candy quickly handed the cart to me so I could push Troy.

"Took you long enough, I hope you got everything off your chest with Rick."

Bonnie started laughing and said, "I'm mad I missed the trophy girl, what's with the Rick thing?"

I shook my head in agreement as Bonnie said, "I'll tell you one thing, Derrick gets better looking with age."

"Yeah, he does," I replied. "He's still a sweetheart too."

My girls knew not to beat me up over our reunion. We all quietly wished it away as Candy showed me her floral arrangements.

When we got outside, Candy took Troy out of the cart while we loaded her trunk. The two of them looked so cute together bonding for Candy's big day. She sucked her teeth and said, "C'mon Troy boy, you need to get your practice in, Lord knows your mama picks you up too much."

Candy was right, I did hold my son too much, but he was everything Alex wanted. I knew that if anything ever happened to his son, he would never forgive me.

Freedom came to me as I began to think about

Derrick again. I put my hands on my hips and thought, "It would have been so nice to spend some more time with him."

By the time I got home it was three o'clock. Troy talked himself to sleep halfway down the parkway and then slept the rest of the way. The minute we got in the door, he unleashed his toddlerhood on me and started tearing up the place. I confined him to one room and let him play with his dinosaurs and jumbo blocks. The constant routine of cleaning up and getting ready for Alex seeped into my blood stream as tension slowly crept up into my head. Bonnie, Derrick and Candy had it made in their "free to go where they damn well please" lives. The routine of chores and taking orders was no different than the shit I used to put up with when I was home. I looked at the front door briefly and then looked at Troy. He was the anchor that kept me from temporarily walking out. I sat down to catch my breath as I thought about my life. *Get up, take a shower, cook breakfast, lay out Alex's uniform, feed Troy, feed Alex, kiss Alex goodbye, walk Alex to the door with Troy on my hip, "Wave bye bye to daddy." Clean up, play with Troy, watch Sesame Street and play with Troy some more. Take him to the park, put him down for a quick nap, take out dinner, clean the bathroom and adjust the blinds for sanity. Chat with Alex and take his lunch order. Wake up Troy, prepare their lunch, feed Troy, put him down for an afternoon nap, feed Alex, sex him up in thirty minutes and tell him you love him....* Fuck, I'm only twenty-one years old, give me a break.

At my age and youthful tenacity, I began to feel like a wind up doll. Seeing Derrick and the girls made spit well up in my throat as I lamented over the thought of freedom. A slight reprieve to my routine came to me in the form of left over food from Troy's birthday party. By the time Alex came in the door, Troy was in his highchair pulled up to the table dropping green peas on the floor.

Alex came home in a good mood and full of small talk. He took a quick shower and changed into some sweat pants and a tank top. After he wolfed down his food like a human vacuum, he pinched his son on his cheeks and kissed his irresistible face. Alex playfully forced his head into Troy's chest while he banged on his father's big head. When Alex grew tired of the joust, Troy threw a handful of green peas on the floor. I immediately grabbed his hand and said, "No Troy, that's not nice."

My adoring son had payback in his heart as he looked at me with two fists and said, "Dehdick!"

The guilty look on my face gave it away as Alex put his detective hat on and said, "What did he say?"

I grabbed a cookie to silence Troy and said, "I don't know."

Alex sat down and quickly pulled me on his lap. The instant I sat down, I could tell the natives were restless. I kissed his lips and said, "Somebody missed me today?"

Alex stroked my back with his heavy hand and whispered in my ear, "We missed you real bad Shanelle."

Troy threw more green peas at the both of us to get our attention. I sighed as my shoulders slumped down in defeat. The two of them vying for my affection was a bit out of hand, but I knew I needed to tend to Troy first to take care of Alex's appetite. Troy reached his hands out to me and said, "Up mamee, up!"

Alex cleared his throat as he hoisted me off his lap and began to walk into the TV room. His feet crushed the vegetables on the floor, which instantly spoiled my stomach. Parts of me wanted Alex, the other half of me wanted to kill him for putting me in this complacent routine.

"C'mon Troy," I said, "Give mommy and daddy at

least fifteen minutes." Troy giggled his way to the floor while I fetched a paper towel. Of course his curiosity led him straight to the mashed up peas on the floor. He held his fingers up and said, "Nasdy!"

I amused him and said, "Yes, that's nasty and dirty Troy," as I wiped him down with the paper towel. Alex turned up the volume on the TV. Perhaps we were making too much noise or he was hinting for me to hurry up. I carried his son upstairs while Troy waved goodbye to his father. He was such a good boy, I was sure he was going to give us twenty minutes. I ran to the bathroom to brush my teeth as Troy babbled in the background, "Dadee, dadee!"

At least Alex had enough sense to quietly come upstairs. I put my fingers to my lips and pointed Alex in the direction of our bedroom. If Troy got wind of his father being upstairs, it would not have worked in our favor.

Alex tiptoed into the bedroom and slid under the sheets. When I walked into the bedroom, an emotional pendulum rocked back and forth between loved and unloved. My heart of hearts told me that he really loved me, but at times it felt like lonely love. I stood in the door way and took off my clothes while he watched me. He sat up and reached out his hand. The part of me that felt unloved began to click like the sound of a musical mobile. A tear swelled up in my eye, but nothing enticed him to ask me what was wrong or if I had a nice day. The smile on his face was my reality. He wanted me and nothing else mattered.

Alex pulled me into his body and moaned as our skin came into contact. He used his right hand to stroke me into a natural arousal. Off in the distance, Troy was spanking his dinosaur in the background exclaiming, "No, no, dino!"

Alex started laughing at his son. He softly caressed my face and said, "He's getting dino back for the way you got on him about those green peas."

Soft pillows and crisp sheets crushed beneath his body while he whispered in my ear and tried to raise our level of intimacy.

"You're a good mother Shanelle. I know that if anything ever happened to me, my son will be okay."

My heart began to flutter up and down like a moth stuck in a net. "Alex don't talk like that, nothing is going to happen to you."

Alex stroked my arm and said, "I know nothing is going to happen to me Shanelle, I just wanted you to know that you're a good mother." He grabbed my face and kissed my lips. I pulled my face away and immediately straddled his hips. Alex placed his arms behind his head and smiled at me.

"What's wrong Shanelle?" he quietly asked.

The pendulum rocked to loved again as I thought about life without him. Desperation became my focus.

"I'm worried about you Alex. I don't know what's going on and you're losing so much weight. Should I be worried?" As I waited for his answer, all I could think about was what Derrick said about my family's safety. Staring intently into his eyes, I searched for an answer. Alex took a deep breath and immediately began to kiss me as my eyes filled with tears. I stopped kissing him and looked at him as they streamed down my face.

"Don't ever say that again, okay?" The tone in my voice was reduced to a plea. My collapse on top of his frame forced him to protect me with a reassuring embrace. Alex's hands pressed my body into his and calmed my temporary fears.

"Shh, shh, baby, stop crying Shanelle, everything is going to be okay." he replied.

Perhaps my emotional weakness was his greatest fulfillment. The pressure of his fingertips rested into my scalp with a gentle massage. He slid them down to my shoulders and lower back with more intensity while I focused on his wonderful touch. Slowly but surely, Alex massaged my stress away with an intimate whisper.

Unknown to Alex's world, when I looked into his eyes, an instant vision of Derrick danced in my head. My heart began to flutter again as I thought his concern for me and my family. Even if I had a direct question for Alex's possible involvement with Steven, I wouldn't dare ask, not ever.

Alex apologized for upsetting me and cuddled my weak heart. Exhaustion from the entire day sank in as he kissed me all over and worked out his own stress. I closed my eyes and let him do all the things that pleased him. My body was filled with pleasure and tension as I turned my face towards the window and contemplated tearing freedom mixed with love into four equal pieces, myself, Alex, Troy and independence. Alex began to moan with quiet intensity. He grabbed my hand and squeezed it tight as he released his love deep inside of me. Listening to him claim me did little for the small glimmers of hope I hid inside my head.

"Don't leave me Shanelle," he stated

"I won't leave you Alex," I whispered.

"I need you Shanelle."

"I know baby," I replied.

"I can't live without you girl," he said breathlessly.

"I love you Alex."

Off in the distance, Troy was tugging and pulling on his sheets. He eventually settled into a quiet nap which gave us more time together. In retrospect, we were lucky to have such a good baby. His sweet disposition allowed us to make love three more times up until Saturday, a day

I shall never forget.

Bloody Wedding Day

Saturday came with full sun and seventy degree temperatures. Troy woke up early that morning so Alex took him for a long stroll on the beach to settle him down for the day. I took full advantage of my time by shaving my legs and packing Troy's diaper bag. When they got back, surprisingly, Alex gave him a bath and put him down for a nap. We discussed our last minute plans for the wedding while Alex took a shower. He told me he was going to shower again at Clinton's house because he knew he was going to get sweaty during the drive. He packed his own bags and flirted with me the whole time. When he finished, he had his hands all over me and I knew I would have to oblige before we left for the wedding. I don't know what revelations came to him at the beach, but while we were in the kitchen, he sat me on his lap and told me that he wanted me to go back to school in the evening while he watched Troy. He picked up the sports section with one hand and looked at me for a response as I kissed his neck in a million places. Alex rubbed my lower back and said, "I want you to go back to school Shanelle, I just wanted my son to have a good start. We were having so much fun at the beach this morning, I started to wonder if you were still having fun."

I responded with a stupid question, but then I caught myself. "But what about the trial...well, I guess you know what's right."

Alex just looked at me and smiled as I began to kiss him again. I didn't need him to go into the particulars, the fact that he brought it up meant that he cared about my needs and wants. I grabbed his hand and he squeezed mine back. Then he picked me up and threw me over his shoulders. Alex spanked me first and it certainly complimented the mood, because I was suddenly feeling like a very naughty school girl. Just like the good old days, we began to play football for lovers. Alex made me play the quarterback and immediately tackled me to the ground. The pillows we threw on the living room floor supported my fall as Alex fell on top of me. I laughed to the top of my lungs as he tickled my stomach and pulled my panties down. He had to cover my mouth twice so Troy wouldn't wake up from his nap. Alex took cool whip and cherries out the fridge and made a sundae out of me as I covered my mouth in complete pleasure. We could hear Troy stirring over the nursery monitor and changed our playful tone to sweet love making so he wouldn't hear us again.

Alex's last words to me were simple.

"This sweet girl of mine."

"That's me."

"Says who?" Alex whispered.

"You baby," I said in a coy tone.

"I like the sound of that."

Alex kissed me for a long time. It was the last kiss we would ever share. If I had known, I would have never left his side on the living room floor.

Preparation for Alex's redemption took place in an abandoned building on Freeway Drive East. Gigi, Rico's hired shooter, stared at the ground and contemplated two techniques for firing the weapon inside the church.

"I think I'm gonna pump it inside the church," she said, as she held it up in the air. "Yeah," she continued, "That's more my style."

Her accomplice took the weapon from Gigi and surveyed it twice, making sure to smooth out the splinters on the handle. Gigi looked into a cracked mirror hanging in the abandoned old room. She scooped her hair up into a ponytail and compared it to Nikki's picture in her back pocket.

"Yeah, we do kinda look alike," she said out loud.

Her accomplice looked up, paused and nodded her head in agreement. Then she placed the sawed off shotgun in Gigi's long duffel bag and said, "Good luck, this one's for us."

Her accomplice couldn't wait for Gigi to get the job done. Flaco promised with a handshake that five thousand dollars would be paid after the hit. Two one way tickets to Miami were in her possession as she held her fist out to Gigi.

Gigi gave her a pound and began to walk out. Mangled debris crushed under her feet as glass and broken needles wedged into the soles of her sneakers. She closed a steel door at the bottom of the landing and began to focus on her hit while her partner stood up to leave on the third floor. Gigi's friend and their tickets to Miami didn't have a chance. A silencer was placed to the back of her head before she could react to the cold steel piece. In one instant, she fell to the floor in a bloody heap.

Gigi awkwardly stepped into a stolen BMW driven by Flaco. He was wearing black leather gloves. Flaco was smart enough to wear them for the get away, but didn't think to wear one when he gave Gigi a picture of Nikki. Gigi noticed the gloves at first, but quickly assumed he didn't want to leave fingerprints in a stolen car. He turned to her and said, "Let's eat first, we still got time before we go to Shiloh."

Candy's wedding arrangements defied perfection. Even though she did most of the planning, Clinton added a special touch of class by ordering four late-modeled Rolls Royces in white. He also requested that the photographer shoot pictures in black and white. As I pulled up to Clinton's house, he was pacing out front like a normal groom on his last day of freedom. Just the sight of Alex calmed him down as I dropped him off. Alex waved with a wink as I drove off with Troy.

Candy and I could barely speak to each other when I reached the church. She knew not to panic even though I was supposed to meet her there an hour earlier. She looked absolutely beautiful and I didn't want to ruin her makeup with my silly tears.

We sat around for an hour as we laughed about the good 'ole days. As I touched up Candy's lipstick, I told her how handsome Clinton looked in his tux. Bonnie poured three glasses of champagne while Candy's mother rolled her eyes at us in disbelief. In friendly unison, two gulps were all we needed as Candy's mother snatched the glass out of Candy's elegant hands and huddled us to the stairwell.

Bonnie walked down the aisle like an elegant swan as a saxophone player serenaded us from the balcony. When it was my turn, Alex eyes widened as I strolled down in my gown. A soft wink from him was our last flirtatious gesture.

Troy came down the aisle to the sound of adoring laughter. He looked like an overstuffed penguin wobbling back and forth in his stubby tuxedo. He occasionally stopped and stared at the people admiring his performance. By the time he reached the front three rows he was pulling on his bow tie with one hand and holding onto the pillow with his other hand. Tammy stood up and coaxed him to stand next to Clinton as the wedding guests quietly clapped for his toddler performance.

The saxophone and clarinet player didn't play the regular wedding march. Instead they played an instrumental version of Luther's *A House is Not a Home*. The entire church was in tears when Candy came down the aisle. It put us all in an enchanted frame of mind as Candy and Clinton exchanged their vows before God. We were so caught up in their romantic kiss, no one except me caught the eye of someone who appeared to be Nikki quickly walking along the pane glass walls of the church. Oddly enough, as she reached halfway down the aisle, God lead my son to toddle to his aunt. I quickly looked at Alex and wondered whether he spotted the mysterious stranger. Unfortunately, his guard was down and while he clapped for Candy and Clinton's intimate kiss, the shooter made her move. She quickly pumped her gun back one time as I opened my mouth to scream. Even though my mouth opened in agonized terror, the sound of the shotgun exploded in the quiet church like a bomb. Alex's massive frame split open in multiple directions as blood splattered against Candy's gown in bright red polka dots. A ten second pause silenced the entire crowd as the shooter hauled ass out of the church. When she jumped in the vehicle her adrenaline was pumping so hard she didn't realize that Flaco had a gun pointed at her head. He fired two shots at point blank range and jumped into a black sedan driven by one of Rico's drug soldiers.

Back inside, family and friends hid underneath the pews for cover as Andre jumped up and ran down the aisle out of the church, followed by Clinton. They stopped dead in their tracks at the sound of a car peeling around the corner. Sunlight pierced directly in his eyes as Clinton bent down to witness Gigi's lifeless body slumped over the passenger seat, while Andre held up his hand like a sun visor to get a visual of the assailants in the getaway car. Andre's mind raced with confusion as he tried to figure out who they were.

Surrounded by an array of white candles flickering at her side, Candy's senses finally kicked in as the tips of her fingers trembled violently to communicate with her husband.

"Clinton no!"

Bonnie's innate thrill for danger and excitement forced her to take off running down the aisle. She caught up with Andre and grabbed him as they surveyed the damage. Andre quickly whispered in Bonnie's ear under the swell of their heavy breathing, "That was Flaco in the car."

Bonnie held her mouth and gasped in disbelief as Andre forced her into silence with a tight squeeze. As for me, I was too stunned to move as the crowd whimpered and cried under the pews. I immediately looked at my screaming son as he held both of his ears like he had a pounding ache in each one. Tammy began screaming her brother's name at the top of her lungs as she held Troy in her arms. Troy was so startled he began to cry as he pressed his fists into his ears. My motherly instinct told me he was stunned but okay as I turned my eyes to my fallen husband. He was slumped on the ground with his massive hands slightly curved resting above his head. I quickly ran to him to talk him through his bloody existence.

"Alex," I said, briefly pausing as the tips of my fingers pressed into his damp bloody tuxedo. My gentle prod had little effect. I changed the tone in my voice to a quiet plea and said, "Alex, wake up baby…Alex please."

No response or movement followed as Candy

began to scream louder. I pressed my lips to Alex's mouth and tried to breathe life into him with a delicate whisper.

"Please Alex, I'm sorry. Don't do this to me and Troy, wake up."

A tear fell off my chin and splashed on his face. Nothing moved him as my knees sat in a pool of his blood. I began to rock slowly back and forth with emotional worry. I picked up his limp arm like I was going to help him get up as one guest began to pray in the distance.

"Oh Lord, please don't test us on this beautiful day."

Her words began to gain momentum as she bellowed out, "Jesus! Jesus! Why?" More guests began to gain composure as I laid across Alex's chest to protect him. The blood oozing from his open wound began to quickly absorb into my dress. While I continued to lay there, a man tried to assist me, but I fought him off.

"Get away from me! Don't you touch me!" Drool escaped my mouth as I quickly wiped it away causing Alex's blood to smear across my cheek and chin. I buried my face in Alex's neck as the sound of sirens quickly came into focus. Bonnie had enough sense and composure to call the police from the pay phone out front. Clinton and his father quickly ushered all the guests out of the church as the sound of rolling wheels and keys jetted down the aisle. Clinton's father came back and had enough strength to pull me off of Alex.

Paramedic number one checked for a pulse, paramedic number two knew what he had to say as he placed his lips to the mouthpiece.

"University, we have a DOA in transit…massive gun shot wound to the chest, black male…"

A loud crackling sound forced us into silence.

"Stand by for Newark P.D."

I reached out to the paramedic and said, "No! You have to take him now. Do something please."

Clinton interrupted the paramedic's response and said in a calm voice, "He's a police officer."

The paramedic paused and then looked at Alex with complete sadness as he pushed the button to speak.

"Please be advised we have an officer down."

The response to the paramedic was quick and steady.

"Do you have an identification? Over."

The paramedic looked at me for a response.

"Alex, Officer Alex Foster!" I yelled.

A stern voice followed.

"Okay, prepare him for transport to University, over."

The paramedic responded, "On our way, over."

My body began to shake all over in small tremors while the four of them counted in unison to lift my sweet Alex on the gurney.

The sound of Troy crying quickly jolted me out of my trance. My poor son was reaching out for me quickly opening and closing his fists. Tammy walked up to me shaking uncontrollably while Troy forced himself out of her sobbing arms. She kept calling her brother's name over and over again in vain. Her anguished tone was reality for all of us. Alex wasn't going to wake up. In fact, he was dead on what was supposed to be a celebrated day. Troy gripped his hands around my neck while Tammy and I followed the stretcher with bellowing sobs. Bonnie met us halfway down the aisle and put her arms around all of us. I looked back as poor Candy stood weeping in her husband's arms. On the most beautiful day in her life, she gained a cherished husband and my husband was gone in an instant.

Tammy's rushed telephone call to her mother was

pathetic. I climbed into the ambulance with Troy in my arms as the world began to move in slow motion. Bonnie snatched the phone from her hand and told Mrs. Foster the horrible news. Tammy briefly gained focus and ran up to the ambulance to get in with me and Troy. The minute she got in, the doors slammed shut and made a rushed exit from the stunned crowd. At least six squad cars flew by us to the chaotic scene. Tammy grabbed onto me and Troy as we huddled together shivering in shock. The paramedic covered Alex's face with a sheet and then began to tend to us.

"Were you hurt?"

We both shook our heads in unison.

"Are you his wife?"

Troy began to reach for his father to no avail.

"Dadee?" He called.

Tammy cried harder into my neck. There was no comfort in listening to Troy beg for his father.

My voice trembled at first, but I had to calm my son.

"Daddy… daddy went night night Troy." I said.

"Ni, night?" Troy asked, as he tugged at Alex's bloody sheet.

"Yes baby, Daddy went night night."

The blaring sound of the sirens was all too surreal as we pulled up to University Hospital. Newark police officers were waiting for our arrival as they stood guard to usher Alex's lifeless body through the double doors. Hospital personnel began to split us up as Alex went one way and we went another way. I ripped myself from the nurses with Troy in my arms screaming for Alex to come back to me.

"Please save him, I'll do anything, please save him!" Troy began to cry all over again as one police officer stopped me dead in my tracks and held me in a tight squeeze. My denial grew faint and weak as more hospital personnel gathered around me.

"Is there someone we can call?"

"Would you like to speak to the chaplain?"

"Your son looks dehydrated, can we get him some juice?"

There was no direction or purpose in their questions. I simply wanted Alex back and I needed to see him. Suddenly, out of nowhere, a familiar voice peeled back the crowd with his hands to get to me. I quickly looked up and found relief in Derrick's eyes.

"Derrick, please, Alex was shot…"

"I know Shanelle, I heard about it in the trauma unit, I'm so sorry…"

I begged for his kindness, "Please take me to him."

"Okay, Shanelle," Derrick said, "Just relax, we'll get you there. We need to get Troy admitted first to make sure he's okay, is that all right?"

He didn't wait for an answer. Instead he took Troy out of my drenched arms and handed him to a nurse. In a calm voice he said, "This is Nurse Sheila Hendricks, she's going to check him from head to toe, he's in good hands."

The confusion and commotion was too much for Troy but I had to let him go. He started kicking violently as the nurse gently stroked his back and soothed him with a soft voice. My eyes immediately searched for Tammy. She quickly shook her head and followed the pediatric nurse down the hall. The warm disposition in Derrick's voice slowed my heart rhythm down and caused my shoulders to relax. Derrick grabbed my blood soaked hand and led me down the hallway as he talked to me.

"You'll be able to observe everything Shanelle, but you won't be able to go inside until they're finished. Even though Alex is…" Derrick paused first and then continued, "Well you have to get cleaned up first to keep the room as sterile as possible." Derrick handed me some tissues and escorted me to a small changing room equipped with a shower.

"Shower off and put these scrubs on when you're finished. After that, I can take you to see him, okay?"

Shock began to settle into my feet and hands. Staring at Derrick with complete desperation in my eyes forced him to put his hands on my shoulders and plead with me.

"Shanelle, listen to me, you need to see him. Go inside and clean up, after that I'll take you to him." Derrick wiped a quiet tear away from my face and said, "Go ahead Shanelle, I'll be right outside this door."

My eyes followed a trail of absorbed blood running down my dress and shoes. I looked at my bloody hands and immediately felt a need to wipe them off.

My warm shower was quick and vigilant as I talked my way through my misery. "He's going to be fine, I know it. He's so strong and brave; God will take care of him. It's not his time yet."

Soap mixed with blood foamed up and slid down my frame. I looked down at my feet as a dark swirl of rich red blood effortlessly flowed into the drain. There was so much blood, I began to wonder how he could survive. Doubt and troublesome voices crept into my psyche.

"It's God's way Shanelle, Alex is dead."

I turned away from the shower stream in denial. More swirling blood accompanied my cries.

"He's not dead! God wouldn't do such a thing!" I immediately turned the shower off and stepped outside to a pure white towel. Left over makeup mixed with blood along my hairline smeared on the fabric. Two strokes at my hairline wiped it away as I quietly began to sob. The realization of seeing Alex's life on me forced me to throw the towel onto the floor and grab another one. I quickly got dressed and walked outside. Derrick stopped pacing and ushered me and the police officer to an observatory room where we could see Alex. Once inside, one look at him confirmed the voices' declaration. Alex was dead.

Derrick and the officer stood back as I slowly walked up to the window. A round bullet was being removed from a gaping wound in his chest. A nurse stood near to receive the bullet with a tray containing four bloody bullets similar in size and shape. There were no monitors, tubes or IVs hooked to him. Dead silence followed and then a loud clang when the last bullet fell to the bottom of the tray. The doctor said a few words to another nurse who quickly jotted some notes. He pulled back his gloves, looked up and motioned Derrick to meet him outside.

Derrick walked out while I peered through the window at my lifeless husband. One tear quickly fell and splashed to the ground. My mouth pressed up against the mirror as vapors quickly formed and disappeared with my breathing rhythms. Derrick walked in with his head held low. He quietly sat me down and began to break the bad news to me.

"Shanelle, I'm so sorry…"

I couldn't bare to hear it from him, so I said it myself. "He's dead right?"

"Yes, he is."

I slowly shook my head and talked away my pain.

"There was nothing they could do to save him right?"

Derrick wiped my tears away and said, "No Shanelle, the impact was immediate, I'm sorry."

I sat up straight and said, "Can I see him now?"

Derrick immediately nodded his head up and down as two tears cascaded down his face in sheer empathy. "Yes, you can see him now Shanelle."

Derrick held the door open for me as I quietly walked inside. A numbing sensation rushed through my body and rested in the soles of my feet again. To the touch, Alex felt cold so I tucked the sheet around him like I always did at home. He looked so peaceful laying there it seemed like the right thing to do to make him feel comfortable. I forced his hand into mine and squeezed it tight.

"Alex, it wasn't supposed to be like this remember?" My fingers softly traced the outline of his eyebrows and hairline. I searched his face for an answer, but nothing came. A sweet memory of the first time he smiled at me flashed before my eyes as nervous laughter escaped from my lips along with pitiful tears. Even thoughts of his sweet redemption couldn't bring him back as I softly said, "You wanted a son and I gave you one…Troy needs you so much, especially now…how am I going to manage without you?"

The stillness in the room caused me to briefly look around as the walls around me began to shrink and close in on us, so I pleaded with him.

"Please Alex, tell me what to do. I'm scared without you in my life." There was no answer. Even a deep sigh from within my soul could not wake him while my hands trembled in unison. My heart felt so heavy and weak I thought I was going to faint. Without thought, I kissed his cheeks, his nose and his closed eyelids.

"I love you Alex, Troy loves you too. Stay with me in my thoughts baby, we need you."

A soft creak in the door forced me to quickly turn around. The Fosters were rushing through the door with misery and loss in their swollen eyes. I only wondered how much time had passed because they lived so far away. This was the first time we gathered together with such heart felt sorrow. Mrs. Foster walked in and fell to her knees as Mr. Foster held me limp in his arms. Derrick touched me on my shoulder and said, "Troy is fine Shanelle, he's sleeping in the pediatric unit when you're ready to see him."

I barely shook my head in response. A mournful and deep wail swelled in my stomach and escaped as I buried myself in Mr. Foster's neck. Derrick quietly walked away and closed the door behind him as my legs and knees buckled beneath me. The sound of Mrs. Foster's mournful crying was the last thing I heard. She lifted her hands up to God and screamed for His mercy. Passing out in Mr. Foster's arms was the right escape from all the madness.

Saying Goodbye

People huddled around my hospital bed with messages of encouragement and hope. Despite the stoic expression on my face, there was nothing they could do except weep for me.

Bonnie stood at my bed crying and wiping snots away while the side of my face rested against a crushed white pillow. Sunlight from the window was the only cue to keep my eyes open as she spoke to me.

"Shanelle, just say something, please. Everything is crazy now. Cops are everywhere, people are calling me about funeral arrangements and I don't know what to tell them. You can't just lay there, you have to do something."

She was my girl, but she couldn't bring Alex back or breathe life into me, so she left with Andre hurt and defeated. After she kissed my cheek, she whispered, "I love you Shanelle and I'm sorry."

My sister-in-law Mary came after Bonnie left. She brought Troy into the room smelling fresh and clean as a whistle with a handful of balloons. Troy banged on the balloons while Mary offered words of encouragement.

"We've been making arrangements for Alex…um, Troy is fine, well you can see that." She picked Troy up and put him on my lap hoping to stir my maternal instinct. Troy smacked my face and put a wet kiss on my neck for his own enjoyment. He serenaded me for a while with a bunch of baby babble.

"Mamee? Mamee!" He gave up when I didn't respond. Mary picked him up and straddled him on her hip again.

"We all need you Shanelle and we love you. Mom and Dad will be here later to pick you up for the funeral tomorrow." She smiled briefly and said, "Don't worry about Troy, he'll be fine." Mary held up Troy's chunky wrist and encouraged him to say goodbye. I never made eye contact with him because he looked just like his father. The minute he began to babble again brought tears to my eyes.

"Mama, night, night?" Troy asked, in a high-pitched tone.

I didn't flinch, but my heart hurt deep inside. Mary didn't answer him. She turned on her heels and quietly walked out the door so I wouldn't see her crying.

After they left, I continued to lay there without the will to get up. As the sun began to go down, Candy and Clinton came for their first visit. Candy was trembling when she walked in. Her eyes widened when she looked at me, but she had enough courage to squeeze my hand.

"C'mon girl, squeeze back, you're stronger than that."

Clinton rested his hand on Candy's shoulder and said, "We don't want you to be alone Shanelle, so if you want to stay with us for a while it's okay, you and Troy are welcome in our home."

Candy squeezed my hand harder and began to cry. Her lips trembled as she spoke. "If you want to be alone, we understand too, but you may want an extra hand with Troy."

I shifted my head to the other side and let go of her hand. I didn't want them, I wanted Alex. Since he wasn't coming back, there was no need to answer her. My immediate rejection forced her face into Clinton's chest for consoling. Clinton tried to coax her out the door, but Candy wouldn't let me get off that easy. She immediately began to give me an update. She said something that made sense and it was straight to the point.

"Alex's obituary was in yesterday's and today's paper. The funeral is tomorrow Shanelle, so you have to snap out of it. Anyway, your son needs you."

I quietly inhaled and let the air flow from my nose. Candy sighed and said, "Okay, you heard me, now I'm going to leave, you know in your heart you have got to get up from that bed."

Clinton patted my hand in a warm gesture before they left. "Call us when you're ready Shanelle, we'll be here."

My eyes followed the door while it quietly closed. Then I shifted my sight to the window. The sound of an ambulance echoed in the distance. A food cart also rolled outside my door as nurses hurriedly talked about their patients. My left hand stretched into the air and forced the sheet off my body. I sat up straight and stroked my hair into place. The hospital scrubs Derrick gave me to wear were riding all the way up my legs and were full of wrinkles. Suddenly there was a quiet knock at the door as Derrick peeked his head through the opening.

"Hey, just thought I'd check on you, today is my last day."

I slowly nodded my head up and down while Derrick pulled a chair to the side of my bed. He looked at my legs dangling from the bed and pointed at my feet.

"That's a good start Shanelle."

Since I refused to speak for the last two days I

needed to clear my throat and sip some water first.

"What?" I asked in a groggy voice.

Derrick pointed to my feet again and said, "At least you've decided to put your feet on the ground, it's a good place to…"

I immediately stood up while Derrick quickly grabbed me to respond to my awkward balance. I looked remorsefully in his eyes and said, "Derrick, can you take me home?"

He grabbed me by the shoulders and waited until I was steady on my feet. He began to focus on my question with strain on his face. Then he looked surprised.

"Sure, I guess I owe you one right?"

"It's a two hour drive," I said, with a blank expression on my face.

Derrick picked up the phone and started to dial. He looked at me, tucked my hair behind my ears and said, "Sure, I'll take you home Shanelle."

Derrick focused on the mouthpiece of the phone and said, "Hi Mrs. Henderson, this is Derrick, listen, I'm going to say goodbye from here, I have to help a friend of mine. Please tell Dr. Johnson that I'll call next week about the research grant." He continued to nod and then hung up the phone. Derrick snapped his fingers and said, "Oh, wait here, you need your bag, it's in the locker."

I walked to the window without responding and stared at the hustle and bustle of life outside. The sight of a young mother pushing a stroller on Bergen Street was my final cue to get home. Alex would want me to be there for Troy.

Derrick quickly came back with my bag and a box for all of my flowers. I grabbed his wrist and immediately said, "I don't want them, give them to the nurses."

Derrick quietly shook his head and held the door open for me as I walked out. The nurses at the station wished me well while I signed my exit form in a wheelchair.

"Take care Shanelle," a kind nurse said, "We'll be praying for you and your family."

I turned and quietly waved without looking back. An orderly tried to assist Derrick with the transport to the lobby, but he refused.

"No chief, she's with me, thanks."

The orderly smiled at the two of us and continued down the hall. He didn't know my circumstances, but he was greatful for Derrick's initiative.

"Man, you didn't even start your residency and I like you already. I hope all the first year residents are like you doc."

Derrick smiled and nodded his head with a quiet thank you. He backed me onto the elevator like a pro and nervously patted my shoulder as I sat in silence. To keep busy on the way down, he searched his pocket for his keys and squeezed them in his hand. When the doors opened, he said, "Okay Shanelle, let's get you home."

The two hour ride home was entertained by the sound of cars flying by with lighting speed. Derrick stayed focused and never took his eyes off the road. I motioned a few turns to him once we got off the exit. When Derrick pulled up, a squad car was parked in front of my house with one officer sitting inside. When he saw me, he quickly jumped out and offered his condolences.

"I'm so sorry for your loss Mrs. Foster, Alex was a great police officer."

He nervously looked at Derrick and quickly shook his hand. I thanked the officer and headed up the quaint pathway in slow motion. White and yellow tulips in full bloom settled my heartbeat as I looked at the front door. Derrick escorted me up the steps and placed my bag on the top landing. He looked extremely uncomfortable and

kept his head down. He stepped back two spaces out of
respect and said, "I'm going back to Cornell on Monday,
but I'll be at the services tomorrow. If you need anything,
my number is in the bag."

When I opened the door, Derrick handed me a
thick envelope and said, "When things settle down, I hope
you have a chance to read this."

When I finally looked at him his eyes pleaded with
me. He began to speak, but suddenly stopped. I quietly
said, "Thank you for taking me home Derrick."

Oddly enough, it felt like deja vu when I said those
words. In a robotic trance, I turned around and walked
inside. My hands settled at my hips as the envelope
Derrick gave me quickly fell to the floor. I slowly looked
around and began to see symbols of Alex everywhere.
Thoughts of him were inescapable as I stroked his utility
belt hanging from the doorknob. Slow steps lead me to the
kitchen where his lingering fragrance rested in my path. I
quickly changed my course of direction and held on to the
banister. The love we made on Candy's wedding day was
evident from the pillows resting carelessly on the floor.
My fingertips touched my collarbone to calm the pain
growing inside my heart. I turned around again and looked
up. I would have paid anything to see him standing at the
top of the stairs waiting for me. His fragrance was the only
thing calling me. One step at a time took me to the top of
the staircase and to the front entrance of our bedroom. I
quietly walked by and took off my filthy clothes. Alex
loved to be clean all the time and I wanted to feel him
after my shower. Once the water began to hit my face, I
began to focus on the things that mattered to him. His
hopes and dreams talked to me while I washed myself.

*"Shanelle, run away with me. Let's take that day
back at the beach and make it ours this time. My heart and
soul is telling me that tonight is our chance and I'm never*

going to let you go."
"I want a son Shanelle."
"All I want is for you to be safe and happy."
"Be good to mommy Pumpy."
"Shanelle, promise me you'll never leave me."
His words were so vivid, I had to respond.

"I promise Alex, I'll never leave you." I turned the water off and dried myself with his towel. I patted my neck and then slowly buried my face in his thick terry-cloth bathrobe while his scent engulfed my senses. He was everywhere I turned, especially in the bedroom. I took his favorite baseball cap off the dresser and put it on my head. After that I put on one of Alex's favorite tapes and laid across the bed on his side. His body was so massive, I could feel the impression in the mattress while my body molded into his frame. My breathing became more intense and with great relief, I finally began to cry for him. My head filled up with enormous pressure but there was nothing I could do but sob. Al Green sent his condolences in one of Alex's favorite songs. I turned over to listen as he soothed me through my agony.

"You make me feel so brand new..." I shook my head as I reminisced about the day I saw him again at the wedding. I wiped the tears from my eyes with our sheets, still touched by the scent of him, while Al crooned another poignant verse, *"I want to spend my whole life with you..."* When I put the sheet down, I noticed a picture of Troy when he was a baby. His smiling eyes were as charming as his father's. I laughed at first and then wiped my nose, relieved that I still had a precious gift from my husband. My body began to ache for both of them as I looked at the clock on the wall. It was just after nine o'clock and I needed to see my son.

Mr. Foster was shocked when he opened the door and saw me standing on his doorstep. Thank God I was wearing Alex's favorite baseball cap because it concealed the puffiness in my eyes. I could hear Troy in the background and I was surprised he was still up when I walked inside.

"Shanelle, uh…when did you get out of the hospital, we were leaving in an hour to pick you up."

His question went unanswered as I walked up to Tammy and snatched Troy from her arms. Anger welled up inside of me as I began to think of the suspicious shooter who looked like Nikki.

"Why couldn't you just listen to him Tammy?" Tammy stood up in complete shock and surprise. Mrs. Foster came barreling downstairs quickly adjusting the belt to her robe.

"What are you talking about Shanelle?"

"Don't play stupid Tammy," I yelled. "Alex warned you about Nikki's family. You damn near fed your brother to them on a fucking plate messing around with Nikki!"

Tammy hurled the next insult. "Me, you got some nerve girl, who's the one hanging out in the projects with Rico. Don't think I don't know either because Nikki told me all about it!"

I looked her up and down and said, "Tammy please, I was watching a damn basketball game. Besides, I bet Rico told her the whole thing. Did you ever think about that? I bet they're on the phone every damn day catching up with my life." I put Troy down and fixed my clothes before I jammed my finger in Tammy's face. "Haven't you heard, payback's a bitch and we all got it with your big ass mouth!"

Tammy leaned back and smacked me violently across the face. Her next comment sent me over the edge.

"You crazy bitch, if Alex never met your demented ass this would have never happened!"

I immediately pushed her to the ground and

gripped my fingers around her throat. Mrs. Foster started screaming and picked up Troy to visually shield him from the altercation. As far as I was concerned, it was going to be a fair fight because Mrs. Foster rescued Troy first, Tammy be damned.

Mr. Foster tried in vain to pry my fingers off her neck, but with one good kick to my pelvic region from Tammy's knee, I was done. Tammy stood up breathing like a bull as she held her red neck and said, "You're as crazy as your fuckin' brother!"

Troy lashed out at her and pointed his finger. "Ti, Ti, not nice!" he shouted.

Even though my face and Kitty were stinging in raw pain, I was glad Troy took up for his pitiful mother. Tammy started crying and immediately ran upstairs.

I ran to the bottom of the landing and grabbed the banister for strength. "Go ahead and cry you fucking baby, I hate you!"

Steven was making a grand appearance in the middle of my tirade while Mr. and Mrs. Foster stood up to me and started yelling.

"Shanelle!" Mrs. Foster said in a high pitched voice, "We're all upset, but don't think you're going to walk in my house and carry on like this, we've all been through hell with Alex leaving us. You don't think Tammy is broken up over this? The papers are making a mockery of our entire family, so it's best we stick together before they rip us apart!"

I backed up from their attack and said, "I'm sorry, but Alex would be here if…"

Mr. Foster placed his hands in the sky as I rehashed the sudden loss of his son. Mrs. Foster walked closer to me and said, "We don't know where Alex would be Shanelle, that was God's plan child."

I snatched Troy from her arms and started heading

for the door. He was the only one in the house who had my back. Mr. Foster quickly stopped me and said, "Why don't you stay here, you don't have to go Shanelle, we can help you with Troy."

I picked up his diaper bag and started to cry hysterically.

"No! I can take care of him myself, I want to go home and be with Alex!" Troy enhanced my sentiment by calling his father's name too.

"Adex! Adex!"

He sounded so cute, but no one was in the mood to entertain him.

Mr. Foster's plea was pathetic. "Shanelle, you're in no condition to drive, at least let me take the two of you home."

I shook my head in denial and said, "No, we'll be fine, you have to stop fixing things all the time, Lord knows I only need to show up for the funeral. You did everything without me, I'm his wife for God's sake!"

Deep down inside, I was glad. I didn't know what to do anyway. It seemed like yesterday that Alex told me nothing was going to happen to him and suddenly he was gone. Mr. and Mrs. Foster put their head down in shame. Tears started streaming down Mrs. Foster's face as she stroked mine for compassion.

"I'm sorry baby, we had to make the arrangements. We couldn't get you to talk for the last two days, we had to do something."

Troy was getting heavy, so I switched him to my other hip. He took my keys from my hand and started gnawing on the leather strap. I yanked it out of his mouth and pacified him by rocking him on my hip.

"What time is the funeral tomorrow?" I asked.

Mrs. Foster rubbed nervously at her upper arms and said, "Eleven thirty." She paused for a minute and then said, "I hope you don't mind, but we bought a suit for Troy to wear." She handed me a small dry cleaning bag with a white suit tailored made for his size. A new pair of Stride Rites were at the bottom of the bag with socks inside. We both stared at each other with tears in our eyes. Troy laid his head on my chest and began to whimper. We quietly stared at the only symbol of Alex left in the world. Mrs. Foster stroked her thumb across Troy's chunky hand and said, "Night night baby, Grandma loves you." After that, she put her arms around me and said, "I'm sorry Shanelle, but we will consult with you from now on. A limo will pick you up at ten thirty to take you to the church." She paused briefly and said, "Did you eat, I have some left over stewed chicken." The look in her eyes was a plea for me to stay sane for her grandson. I couldn't recall the last time I ate, so I accepted a wrapped plate to go.

Mr. Foster quietly picked up his keys and followed me out the door. Even if I didn't want him to follow me, he would have followed me anyway. Troy was fast asleep by the time I put him in his car seat. I decided not to roll the windows down just to keep Alex's scent with me. At this point, I decided to be stoic and tough it up. I wasn't really on my own, but I knew that I didn't want everyone telling me what to do and where to go.

Your Love is King, by Sade followed me home as tears streamed down my face. I wiped them away at a traffic light as I continued to stare straight ahead into night. I would have done anything to have Alex driving the car and telling me what to do next, but it wasn't going to happen.

I let Mr. Foster carry Troy in the house. When I took Troy from him he said goodnight and quietly left.

Troy went right back to sleep after I changed his pamper. I looked around his room for a minute and finally turned off the lights. Troy tossed and turned for a second and then found his comfort zone by rubbing his blanket. He exhaled real hard and was off in his own dream world.

I walked into the bedroom and changed into one of Alex's tee shirts. He had enough to last a lifetime. I adjusted his baseball cap on my head and turned on the TV. Reality quickly came into focus as soon as Eyewitness News reporter, Carmen Rivera appeared. She was standing outside the Garvey Projects with a microphone in her hand.

"I'm currently at the Garvey Street projects as North Orange police detectives question various people about the female assailant who shot Detective Alex Foster at Shiloh Haven Baptist Church on Saturday. Sources tell us that the shooter was fatally shot after she got into a stolen black BMW. The shooter of the female assailant jumped into another get away car. Newark Police are currently combing the car for possible fingerprints. A source close to Detective Foster's wife said the female assailant was able to enter the church without suspicion because she looked strikingly familiar to Nikki Rivera. Interestingly enough, Nikki Rivera, is the sister of federal inmate Rico Rivera, who is currently under indictment for various drugs and weapons offenses stemming from the Garvey Projects. The twist in this story Bill is that Nikki Rivera and Tammy Foster, the sister of the murdered detective have been intimately linked as college roommates at Pitt University. Most people are speculating that this was a form of retribution to the drug and gun bust that happened here at Garvey."

I squeezed my eyes tight as the pieces to the puzzle began to fit together. The reporter paused for a minute and motioned her hand to a disheveled man standing in the background. "We have one brave resident of Garvey who may have some information."

Upon sight, I immediately stood up with my mouth wide open. The minute he began to speak, I knew it was my guardian angel from the past. It was Quadir, the guy who used to torment me at Roy Rogers. He also saved me from those thugs who tried to rape me. Quadir snatched the microphone from Carmen's hand and started mumbling.

"Yeah, uh, uh, uh, uh, um, looka here, uh, I don't mean no harm. We's good folk, you know, just trying to make a livin'."

Quadir paused to wipe the white pasty residue from his mouth, as I looked at him with compassion for the kind act he bestowed upon me so long ago.

"Yeah, like I was trying to say... uh, we love da police."

Carmen snatched the microphone from Quadir's hand and said, "Thank you sir. As you can see, there is sentiment here in Garvey, but this investigation is certainly not over. Back to you Bill."

I turned the TV off and quickly rolled on my back.

"Be strong Shanelle, you can do this," I said to myself. I picked up the phone and called Candy. She was relieved I left the hospital.

"Who took you home?" She asked.

"Derrick," I whispered.

"Derrick?" she asked, in a surprised manner. Then she asked, "Where's Troy?"

"Sleeping," I replied. I paused briefly and said, "I'm sorry that had to happen on your..."

Candy cut me off and said, "No, I'm sorry for you Shanelle, I'd give anything to see you with Alex."

I couldn't respond. I wanted to tell her about Nikki and all the confusion at the Fosters. The thought of Alex not turning the key in the lock made everything else go away.

"I'll see you tomorrow then okay?" I asked.

"Of course you will Shanelle," Candy said.

With what little strength I had, I rolled over on Alex's side of the bed and set the alarm. Tears began to fall again so I picked up the teddy bear he gave me on our first date and crawled back into bed with Alex's baseball cap on my head. Numbness settled into my joints as I drifted off to sleep.

One hour later, Troy woke up crying for his father. I picked him up and walked back and forth on our quiet hardwood floor to settle his nerves. Nothing I seemed to do worked until I let him sleep in our bed. Troy rubbed on the sheet for fifteen minutes while I stared at him. He finally settled down and drifted back to sleep. I didn't want him to start picking up bad sleeping habits so I put him back in his crib after twenty minutes. A quick glance at the clock forced my eyes to close once I climbed back into bed. I turned to his side and said, "Goodnight Alex."

They Come and Go

Without fail, a limousine picked us up and we were escorted to Metropolitan Baptist Church in Lakewood for Alex's funeral. News reporters and well-wishers from near and far lined up in front of the church, somberly looking through the car windows at any glimpse of the family.

When I stepped out of the limo, flashing cameras immediately lit up to take a picture of the fallen officer's wife. Mr. Foster escorted us behind Alex's maple and gold encased coffin. Flowers filled the church in every direction as the weeping audience stood up to receive us. Quiet whimpers and sniffles passed us by while we walked down the aisle. I held Troy tight in my arms and patted his back sensing that he would quickly fall asleep once everyone was seated. He woke up three more times crying for his father and we were both weary from the ordeal.

A young man from the balcony sang *His Eye is on the Sparrow,* while we slowly positioned ourselves to our seats. Mr. Foster sat in between me and Mrs. Foster, but Mrs. Foster was in greater need of his embrace as she began to wail for her precious son.

She lifted her hands to the heavens and screamed, "Lord Jesus! You should have taken me! Not my son, not my son heavenly Father!"

An usher quickly rushed to her side and fanned her flushed face as the reverend began to speak.

"Trust in Him and He will not lead you astray. Let the church say amen." The audience rang out his request, *"Amen!"*

"Today is a day that I stand before you to provide funeral services for the Foster family. Now, it is not too often that I have to provide services for parents who have lost a child. So I ask you today to trust in Him and He will not lead you astray. Now, y'all ought to know that I watched Alex Foster grow up in this very church. He comes from a good God fearing home with parents that have worked their entire lives to watch their children become wonderful adults. In my time here, I watched this child of God grow from an infant to a young boy and then a man. And if it were not for his family's faith and Alex's love of the Lord, I don't think Alex would be in peace right now. But you are going to have to trust me when I say that Alex is in a better place. No matter how hard that sounds, no matter how many nights you weep, if you trust in God, he will not lead you astray. Now, I'm gonna ask that you pray for this family, especially his young wife and son. Alex may have left us a little too soon, but faith will be with us every day of our lives. His son, his wife and his family need our prayers during this difficult time. Not even the devil's bullet can stop our faith in the almighty Father...

Troy's head became heavy on my shoulder so I laid him across my lap while the reverend continued. The words devil and bullet quickly disconnected me from the service. I looked at Mr. Foster and offered him a soft smile while Mrs. Foster cried on his shoulder. Candy looked surprised when I turned around to look at her in the distance. Oddly enough, just behind Candy sat my father in a black single-breasted suit. He was sitting all by himself and I wondered whether Mrs. Viv was with him or home tending to Steven.

Before the final procession took place, an officer handed me the American flag and Alex's police photograph. I handed it to Tammy as a gesture of forgiveness. She looked at me and wiped her tears away as we stood up. I kept my eyes focused on the ground until I got to the limo. Looking at people only made it worse.

Everything felt hollow and empty until we got to the gravesite. There was a massive crowd around us to wish Alex farewell. As we gathered in our seats under the tent, a quiet commotion took place behind us for everyone to see. To my embarrassment, Mrs. Viv and my cousin Marvin were struggling to hoist Steven down from his handicap ramp while he sat in his wheelchair. A few good men gathered around to help them as my father quietly took over. To my surprise, Mrs. Viv politely pushed him away and accepted the help of strangers as Steven rolled down the ramp with an eight-inch lobster bib tied around his neck. The Fosters didn't know what to make of the commotion. I just closed my eyes and tried to wish them away.

"Why did she have to bring him?" I thought to myself. To make matters worse, he was babbling more than Troy making Godzilla versus Rodan noises above the crowd. With Marvin and Mrs. Viv at his side wiping his mouth, there was no way I was going to forget Alex's funeral.

It was considerably cool that day and I was relieved the crowd dispersed quickly. A few well-wishers walked up to me to express their condolences, including Derrick. Mrs. Viv watched me from a cautious distance while Derrick softly pressed my body into his chest for a final hug goodbye.

"I'm so sorry Shanelle, I hope you find the strength to keep moving. In my heart, I know you will."

Mrs. Foster looked at the two of us with curious eyes and quietly walked away. When Derrick walked away, my father walked up to me with open arms.

"Wow, look how big Troy is getting." He seemed a little embarrassed because it was the first time he saw his grandson. My father quickly changed the subject to avoid his own guilt. "I couldn't leave without saying goodbye Shanelle. I'm sorry about your loss."

The past didn't matter after he said he was leaving. There was so much between us that needed to be said after all this time.

"Leaving for where?" I asked.

"North Carolina," he replied. "Well, Viv and I decided to split for a while… it's for the best."

I was so shocked I put Troy down as he immediately clutched my leg. "Well, don't go just yet, we need to talk." My eyes quickly shifted back and forth. "Why don't you stay at my place, just for the night so we can talk dad."

He searched my eyes for a second, paused and then said, "Ok, but I'll get on the road in the morning."

Mrs. Viv's hurried steps almost knocked Troy over with Steven's wheelchair.

"Ma, be careful!" I said as I shielded Troy from Steven. Even though he was no longer a threat, there was no remorse in my heart. Mrs. Viv tried in earnest to appear concerned.

"Oh, I'm sorry, I almost hit my grandson. Look at him with his handsome self." She looked at all of us and said, "Shanelle, I'm so sorry about your loss, I hope Alex left you well so you don't have to struggle anymore."

She might as well have thrown a dagger at me and pushed me in the hole right next to Alex with her unsympathetic statement. The Fosters huddled together and stared at my freak of nature family while I tried to split everyone up.

"Listen, the repast is back at the church mom. Dad, you can follow me back to the house if you want."

He quickly shook his head and said, "That's fine with me."

Marvin's mouth began to salivate as soon as he heard the word repast. Food was just around the corner as he gasped for breath and pulled on Mrs. Viv's arm.

"Let's go Vivian, I'm hungry. Bye Shanelle." Before she pushed Steven away, Mrs. Viv firmly grabbed my wrist and gripped her nails into my skin. The force of her grip and the pain piercing into my skin frightened me for a second or two. In a demonstrative voice she said, "Whatever he tells you, I'll always be your mother." After that, she released my wrist by pushing it away. I immediately looked at my father. He put his head down in shame and began to walk away. Mrs. Foster found the break she was looking for and walked up to us.

"Shanelle, are you coming, the limos are leaving," she asked patiently.

I looked at my father and said, "No, go ahead, I'll get the car seat out and ride back with my father."

Confusion set in as I began to wonder why none of them attempted to introduce each other. Perhaps I distanced myself from them so much, it only seemed like the right thing to do. Mrs. Foster looked disappointed, but I knew she would understand. Candy, Clinton and Bonnie walked up to me and gave me a group hug. Candy spoke first.

"We're going to get back on the parkway, Clinton has a flight going out at four. If you need anything Shanelle, just give me a call."

Bonnie squeezed me tight and forced back her

tears. "Andre sends his condolences Shanelle, if you need anything, just call me."

I nodded my head and walked them back to their car while my father started up his vehicle. He helped me put Troy in the car and strapped him into the car seat. He looked agitated and nervous. I only wondered what would come next.

Revelations

I was glad my father accepted the invitation to go back to the house. It kept my mind off the real issues even though I wasn't ready for new ones. I showed him the guest room and offered him a washcloth and towel to freshen up. He extended so many compliments on my house that I began to get nervous about catching up with him. I knew he had to tell me something because he looked distant and worried.

Troy ate a few bites of his sandwich and was ready for another nap. Once he fell asleep, I changed into some sweats, made a sandwich for my father and poured juice for the both of us. He looked like all of his energy left his body. When we sat down at the table he could barely look at me. His eyes shifted to his hands while he caressed his drink.

"Dad," I asked, "Tell me, what is it?"

He sipped some of his juice and searched my eyes for a place to start. I got up and sat closer to him. Maybe it relieved the pressure of looking me straight in the eyes but he began his story.

"Shanelle, I want you to know that I am sorry for everything that happened to you. I feel like such a failure for not looking out for you the way a father should. I've been carrying this guilt with me for so long, I guess there's never going to be a good time to tell you." He paused to pick up a napkin and wiped his hands and brow. "Today is probably not the best day to tell any of this to you, but Vivian was determined to come here and ruin whatever peace you may have left."

My heart began to pound in multiple repetitions. Whatever it was, it must have been pulling at my father's heart for so long, he looked like he had to let it go. We sat next to each other in silence until I made the first move. I stared out the window as a puffy white cloud drifted along against the backdrop of the bluest sky. The strain in my heart became heavier and heavier, but the moving cloud was my cue to keep moving forward.

"Dad, just tell me, start from the beginning." Even though I gave my father the green light to speak, I began to drift off with the cloud while I spoke to Alex.

"I guess a resurrection is impossible, huh Alex?"
"You're right baby it's impossible."
"Can you believe my father is here with me?"
"I can believe it baby, he's got something heavy on his heart, listen to him and find your way, I'm with you baby."

I put my hand on top of my father's hand as he began to tell his story. He cleared his throat. It must have been a heavy burden because I could see his Adam's Apple move slowly down and rise back up again. When he opened his mouth to speak, I began to stare out the window again.

"When Vivian and I got married, we were anxious to have children right away. It was her dream to have a houseful of children. After Steven was born, we waited a year to have another child. Unfortunately, Vivian had three miscarriages, one after the other. She was so driven to have another baby it became an obsession Shanelle." He took a deep breath and turned his glass in slow circles. "She blamed me for everything and it definitely put a strain on our marriage. I buried myself in work and started coming home late just to avoid her. She made such a fuss over Steven because he was the only thing that could keep her mind off of getting pregnant again." My father sighed at first. I knew something big was coming so I touched base with Alex again.

"I don't think I'm ready for whatever it is he's going to tell me Alex."

"You'll be fine, I'm here."

"Vivian put on so much weight, the doctor told her that she would be better off losing fifty pounds before she tried again."

I was curious at this point. "So what happened, she got pregnant with me?"

Serious strain became him again before he continued. This time he blurted it out. "Shanelle, I had an affair with another woman, Vivian's not your mother."

My fingers became limp on the table. What little light shining through the window began to fade out and darken the room.

"What do you mean she's not my mother?" My voice cracked underneath the swell of my own question. Small beads of sweat formed around my hairline.

My father put his hands up and folded them in front of his mouth. "Please let me finish Shanelle, or I'll never get this off my chest." He folded his hands on the table and continued.

"I had an office affair with a woman named Clara. It only lasted a year, but before I knew it she was pregnant with you Shanelle."

"What!" I screamed.

My father immediately began to shake his head in

his own denial. "Shanelle, I'm sorry, but I have to tell you this. Vivian is not your mother, but she accepted you because…"

I immediately stood up and covered my ears. "Stop this daddy, why are you doing this to me?" My father jumped up and said, "Vivian is not your mother, but she raised you like you were her daughter."

I got up to walk out the kitchen, but he stopped me in my tracks. "I'm sorry Shanelle, your mother died in a car accident when you were two weeks old, I had to tell your mother, uh, I mean Vivian, well she is your mother, she raised you… well, the truth is, there was no one else to take care of you but me and Vivian."

"Why are you doing this to me!" I yelled. "I just buried my husband for God's sake!"

He began to shake uncontrollably and said, "If I didn't tell you, Lord knows Vivian was prepared to do it today. I'm sorry Shanelle, she never forgave me for the affair and I just couldn't take it anymore. She tried to blame you for Steven's paralysis and I couldn't let her do that to you."

"Me!" I yelled, "I didn't do anything to him, he brought that on himself daddy!"

He shook his head in agreement and said, "You're right Shanelle, but there's no convincing her because of what I did so long ago. She accepted you because of her faith, but she just couldn't forgive me or accept you as her own."

I folded my arms as my father looked down at my hands. My wedding ring was the only ornament on my fingers. He looked puzzled at first and then looked at my right hand. Tears began to form in his eyes as he looked at my right hand ring finger.

"Your ring," he said, and then paused. "Where is the ring I gave you?"

Years of sweltering one-sided memories festered in my brain as I exploded.

"The ring, you're worried about that damn ring?" I wiped my tears away and went off.

"I did exactly what you said daddy. I kept myself pure until the man of my dreams swept me off my feet! But trust me, I ran to him out of desperation and safety. Thank God he was a good man in his heart. You did nothing to protect me. For years you went to work while she whipped my ass and stroked Steven's ego. I cooked and cleaned up Steven's filthy habits while you looked the other way, busy on a train to New York, hoping that dear Mrs. Viv wouldn't throw you out. Look where it got me, locked up in closets, walking the streets, beat up and trying to survive. No wonder none of you came around when Troy was born! I'm real easy to forget. What was I to you, some fucking sacrifice for your adultery? I hate you!"

My screaming must have startled Troy because he immediately began to cry. I ran upstairs to settle him down but he wouldn't go back to sleep. The last thing he needed to hear was instability in my voice. His last few days were filled with sounds of anguished crying and heartache. I walked the floor with him again and sang to him in a trembled voice.

"*Yes, Jesus loves me, yes Jesus loves me, because the bible tells me so.*" He settled down, but he gripped my shirt and refused to be placed on the floor. By the time I came downstairs with Troy in my arms, the front door was ajar. The sound of a car peeling off in the distance caught my attention. My father was long gone, suitcase and all. I held onto Troy for comfort and used my foot to slam the door shut. Silence overwhelmed the room until Troy gave me new energy.

"Dadee? Dadee go bye bye?" He pointed to the

door and then put his finger in his mouth to soothe his gums.

"No baby, that wasn't Daddy, Daddy went to heaven."

Troy stared at me puzzled. The word heaven was a new vocabulary word that he had yet to use or master.

"Headen?" He asked in a squeaky tone.

"Yes, baby daddy went to heaven, but he's with us."

I put Troy on the floor and held his hand to guide him into the kitchen for something to drink. I fought back tears and cleared my throat from the explosion in my head. Troy picked up an envelope off the floor and handed it to me. I knew it was Derrick's letter, but I wasn't ready for condolences. I placed it carefully in our letterbox for another day. Suddenly, the doorbell rang. The stranger in the window could have been a member of the press, but I didn't sense it when I opened the door.

"Good afternoon, are you Shanelle Foster?"

"Yes," I replied. "I'm Shanelle Foster."

He smiled and then paused before he passed a business card to me. "My name is Neil Harrison from Prudential. I'm your husband's insurance agent."

His suit and business card looked official so I let him in the house. A squad car was still parked out front so I wasn't worried. I directed him to the kitchen and offered him some coffee.

"I'm sorry," he said as he laid his briefcase on the kitchen table. "I can't stay very long, I have a few stops along the way."

I sat down next to him while he took an envelope out of his briefcase. Troy clamored alongside me and then plopped himself on the floor with one of his favorite toys. The insurance agent smiled at him and then looked at me.

"Mrs. Foster, I'm sorry about your loss, I know this

is a difficult time for you, but your husband left specific instructions with his father to make sure you received the proceeds of his life insurance policy immediately upon death."

Mr. Harrison placed the envelope on the table along with an application. "You also have insurance on the house. Once this form is filled out, your mortgage will be free and clear."

He stood up and exclaimed in a rushed tone, "Your husband left you well off Mrs. Foster. I know the money won't replace him, but at least you'll be able to provide for yourself and your son." He began to head for the door and said, "Call me if you have any questions."

The visit was so abrupt I didn't know what to say except, "Uh, okay, thank you, Mr. Harrison." When I walked back into the kitchen, Troy was pulling on the refrigerator. I knew he was hungry so I grabbed some Cheerios out of the storage jar and sat him in his high chair. I gave him a cup of juice and more cereal to entertain him. I sat at the table and slowly opened the envelope. The check from Prudential looked like a practical joke, but it had my name on it and Four Hundred and Fifty Thousand Dollars written in the box. I quickly put it down and looked at the numbers written in the box again along with the written amount. It said the same thing, "Four Hundred and Fifty Thousand Dollars." I looked at Troy feeding himself and said, "I can't believe it." A phone call to the Fosters confirmed my doubt. Mr. Foster took his time and talked to me even though he was heart broken.

"I didn't think they would come today Shanelle, but that's what my son wanted." He sniffled a little and said, "I have another check for Troy from his father too. We spent our lives saving money in case we ever had to go to court for that thing in Virginia, but I guess it's over now."

"Well why don't you keep it," I replied. Mr. Foster
quickly responded. "No Shanelle, I gotta follow Alex's
wishes to the letter. He loved you so much and you have
to make sure that Troy is taken care of, that's all he wanted
for the two of you." I held on to the phone cord like it was
a lifeline to Alex.

There was a napkin in my pocket just to catch my
tears. "I know and I will," I replied.

Mr. Foster cleared his throat among his sniffles and
said, "What's my grandson doing?"

"He's eating, as usual," I replied.

"Well," Mr. Foster said, "You know we have plenty
of company here. You and Troy are welcome to come if
you get lonely." Without thinking I answered him like a
real daughter should answer any father. "Thanks Dad, I
love you."

"We all love you Shanelle, come by later on
okay?"

"Okay, I will."

I hung up the phone and walked up to Alex's make
shift office. The check went into a mail slot for deposit. So
much happened in one day, I was beginning to feel sleepy.
Troy just had a nap so I decided to put him in his playpen
while I rested on the floor. I sang his favorite song to him
while he held on to my arms going up the stairs.

*"Whoa, whoa, sweet thang, don't you know you're
my everything."* Chaka couldn't have coined a sweeter
phrase than that. Troy sang back to me in his own lullaby
while he chewed on his finger. Then he put his finger in
my mouth so we could sing together.

"Ma, ma, ma, ma." Troy sang.

"Yes, mama is your sweet thang," I said, as I laid
him in his playpen. He sat up and grabbed his toys.

"Be a good boy for mommy while I take a nap." I

stared into his charming eyes and laid on the floor. It wasn't long before I drifted off to sleep. A stage of grief took place in the form of a dream. It must have rested there until today. Never had I been faced with such despair, happiness and hopelessness.

A soft shade of light began to shine in a six by six foot padded room as the voices from my past and present gathered for my mental case management conference. My dear friend Nemesis appeared from deep inside my conscience wearing a tight full-length red dress. Her hair was slicked back in a ponytail with a fully bloomed white flower tucked behind her ear like Billy Holiday. She took a seat at the head of the table and quietly lit a cigar with her head cocked to the side to enhance her sophisticated demeanor. In a sultry voice she said, "Bring her in boys."

The Big One and the Meek One pulled the curtain back with their grubby hands and pushed my chair out from behind a black velvet curtain. My mouth was covered with duct tape and I was confined to a crisp white cotton straight jacket. Desperate pleas of help were muffled behind the thick sticky tape as my head thrashed back and forth.

"Okay," Nemesis said, "Let's bring this meeting to order." Nemesis put the cigar in her mouth and spoke while it bobbed up and down.

"Let's face it Shanelle, I did a good job at keeping Derrick out of your pants, so we can't blame him, he certainly loves you." She looked around at her cohorts and said, "Did you see the way he handled himself at the hospital? Shanelle couldn't ask for a better man. He's so caring, confident and more importantly, she'll be safe. I don't think anyone would have a need to hunt him down like a wild animal. Alex must have really done some dirt behind that badge to get popped like that." Nemesis removed the cigar from her mouth and pressed her lips

together to contain her worry. She sighed briefly and said, "I guess we'll never know."

Suddenly she smiled and looked me in the eye. With a sweet tone in her voice she said, "Shanelle, you should open the letter. You're working my nerves already; dropping it here and there. Troy is going to need a father and as for you... well an empty bed is no place to be on a cold winter night. You know winters are rough on you with the whole Steven thing."

The Meek One covered his mouth and giggled as he held my face still. Nemesis looked down at the table and picked up the infamous photograph of me the day Alex broke my virginity. Tears streamed down my face as I thought about our three days of love. Nemesis looked at me sternly and said, "Girlfriend, that was a vicious photo you took. Steven did a good job of running you out of that house and right into Alex's loving arms. Don't get me wrong, he was a good man, but a little too controlling. We won't blame him, but he sure had a way of stressing you out."

The Big One hurled an attack at me. "Yeah, she can throw down can't she, peanut butter, toothpaste, yogurt..."

Nemesis put the cigar back in her mouth and held her hand up in my defense.

"Now, now, Steven, Mrs. Viv and Dear Daddy sure did a number on her, nobody can deny that. But the real question is, can she forgive and just let that shit go?"

The Little One started growing fangs out of sheer anger and growled, "Hell no! Let's light a fire, torch the damn house, throw rocks at it, better yet..." The Little One turned my face into his demonic eyes and said, "Go ahead and kill yourself, then you'll never have to worry again!"

I rocked my head out of his hands and looked at

Nemesis with a quiet plea of strength. Nemesis understood me and said, "No, not Shanelle, she's too strong, she's a fighter, just wait and see." She put out the cigar and crossed her hands. "You're not going to leave that precious boy behind without his mother. Your own mother did that to you in a tragic accident. Troy deserves to know you and love you. He also needs a father and Derrick is right there waiting for him."

Troy managed to hit me with one of his toys. It wrestled me out of my dream and startled my senses. I smiled at Troy's infantile laughter as he held his hands up to take him out of his confinement.

I looked around the room and then looked at Troy. His eyes were as handsome as his father's. He stood on his tippy toes for me to pick him up and I obliged, thinking of the crazy dream I had. Suddenly, a message from Alex came to me like a day gone by from my past, "Get organized Shanelle."

Rico's Way

Rico was so impressed with Flaco, he had to call him to give him his props.

"Yo man, your shit was smooth like that, I gotta give you credit."

Flaco bobbed his head in agreement and said, "Yeah, yeah, right, right."

Rico took a drag from his cigarette and threw it to the ground. He used his brand new white Nike sneaker to crush the lit embers in front of him. "Call Nikki and tell her not to go back to Pitt. She needs to be by my side with Mommy and Papi for the trial. Oh yeah, tell her to drop Tomboy Tammy and start hanging out with the fellas, she needs to be around family now. Last but not least, send Gigi's mother some money for the funeral and a nice arrangement, we owe them that much."

"Aight, I'll take care of it," Flaco replied.

Three days later, Nikki called Tammy to let her know she was picking up her stuff from the dorm room.

"But why, just finish this semester," Tammy pleaded.

"No, I gotta be with my family right now baby, they need me."

"But I need you," Tammy said.

Nikki sighed and said, "Things are crazy right now, so I think we should lay low for a while."

Tammy went to the refrigerator for some deli meat and said, "How long?"

Before Nikki hung up she said, "I'll let you know."

Tammy hung up and buried her sorrow in three sandwiches, Doritos and two Sunkist sodas. She took two bites at a time before she swallowed and wiped her tears away. Mrs. Foster stood in the doorway and watched her daughter's quiet torment take place. When Tammy reached for the last sip of soda, Mrs. Foster finally said, "Do you feel better now?" Tammy stood up, threw the can in the garbage and said, "Leave me alone, mom, suddenly Shanelle is a damn angel, just because Alex is gone. What about me, I miss him too and it wasn't my fault!" Mrs. Foster rubbed Tammy's back while she wept for her lost brother and girlfriend.

"Tammy, it's going to take time to heal. You're going to pick yourself up and keep moving. If you want to take a semester off that's fine, but it's best that you go back to school and continue your regular routine."

Before Tammy went back to school, Mrs. Foster gathered everyone for dinner to discuss our grief. Despite the tension in the room between me and Tammy, we all agreed that it was best to resume our lives without any comments to the press. Mr. Foster hired an attorney to be our spokesperson during the trial. For our own personal safety, we decided that being in the public eye was the wrong move. Luckily the police had a good tip on Alex's murder. Unknown to any of us, Andre, the entrepreneur had a keen sense of eyesight and a strong scent for the smell of reward money. Without a word to anyone, he was secretly working with the police to nail Flaco for Alex's murder. Fifty thousand dollars from crime stoppers had

Andre's mouth watering for legitimate money to start his own business. It wouldn't be long before Andre collected his reward.

Even if Rico thought things were going his way, it didn't work out in his favor. The trial lasted five months and he was sentenced to thirty years under the toughest federal sentences. Racketeering, money laundering, extortion and witness tampering followed his demise, while Mama Barb picked up a fifteen-year bid. Poor Mookie wept like a damn fool in front of the news cameras. His so-called basketball career was over in the blink of an eye. The stress of the trial sent him into a weed and drinking binge just like Steven. Without the academic smarts and his mama to back him up, life was too unbearable, so he moved to Maryland with his aunt.

Amazingly, Garvey began to flourish with green grass and a small community garden. A few residents banded together to form a community watch project. Under the watchful eye of the North Orange police, peace came again in the form of happy children laughing under the early twilight with fewer junkies around. Quadir still hung around. He watched parked cars at night and informed the community group when suspicious people were loitering in the complex. A few tenants brought him some decent clothes and taught him how to read at the North Orange Public Library. Alex may have thought differently, but they were really decent people just trying to survive.

My Turn

Seventeen months passed me by and I was still in the thickest stage of denial. Jack kept me posted on the murder investigation but parts of me felt like he was keeping information from me. To keep my mind busy, Mrs. Foster convinced me to drop Troy off for the day just so I could go through the mail. He was a happy and well adjusted two year old with a doting mother by his side. Troy spent plenty of time with his grandfather, which made up for some of his father's absence. Candy agreed to come over and sort months of mail that piled up in the kitchen. Jack also agreed to come over and go through Alex's clothes for the homeless. I considered it a good start. Everything Alex owned was neatly in its place. The pillows we threw on the floor from our last interlude were still laying on the floor. Troy made a few adjustments, but I forbade him from going in the living room.

Jack said very little when he came. He and Alex were so close, it was difficult for him to organize his belongings. Alex's badge, hat and smaller incidentals were placed in a keepsake box for Troy. All of his other belongings were eventually boxed up and hauled away. Jack met me at the bottom of the stairs for a hug goodbye.

I grabbed his wrist when he reached the bottom of the stairs. I wanted him to tell me more about Alex since there was so much controversy during the trial and investigation. He seemed insulted that I asked and pulled me into the kitchen while Candy went to the bathroom.

"Look around Shanelle, he was a good police officer and a good husband. There's no sense in you trying to figure out anything else, just hold on to your memories okay?" Jack pressed his fingertips into my shoulders when he finished. A quick glance in his eyes suggested there was something more, but if there was, Jack wasn't going to tell. When I looked down, he promised he would call, but I knew he was lying. I held on to him for a little while and then stared into his eyes again for closure. I opened my lips to speak but nothing came out. Jack grabbed me by the hand and said, "Remember what I said, he was a good man. Troy ought to grow up and learn the same thing." He sucked his teeth and said, "Listen, I better run, you take care okay?"

He could barely fight back the tears as he left with Candy standing by my side. When the door shut behind him, we went back upstairs to survey the damage. Empty hangers were slowly swinging back and forth. A cool breeze whistled underneath the opening from the window and forced clean air into my lungs. The hangers began to clang together like the soft tones of church bells on Sunday morning. Candy quietly looked at me and held my hand.

"C'mon," I said, "We can let the bedroom air out while we open the mail."

Candy and I went into the kitchen. She quietly picked up the phone to see what Clinton wanted for dinner. Her voice sounded calm and relaxed as they exchanged messages of love to each other. I think the tragedy they experienced solidified a perfect bond of matrimony. I looked out the window and wished I had Alex around to talk to me. It was something I sorely missed. When I did talk to him, the words never came back. They followed me in nature's smallest gifts; an ocean breeze, morning birds or leaves cascading to the ground. Candy looked me in the eye and sensed my longing the instant she sat down.

"So what about you? Don't you think it's time?"

I picked up a stack of mail and passed it to her. "Separate them first and then we'll open it."

Candy quickly went through the mail and picked up one that stood out among the rest.

"This one doesn't have anything on it except your name."

I looked at Candy and quickly put my head down.

"I know, Derrick gave it to me the day before Alex's funeral."

Candy perked up a bit and said, "How come you didn't open it?"

I looked down at my checkbook and recorded the balance from my cable bill. Candy began to tap the envelope on the table for a response.

I quickly looked up and said, "Because, I didn't want to read it."

Candy's face looked strained and confused. "Shanelle," she said, "It's been…"

I finished her sentence. "Yeah, seventeen months to be exact since Alex died."

Candy put her elbows on the table and clasped her hands together. "Shanelle, I'm not asking anything, just see what he has to say. If you didn't care, you would have thrown the letter away. But you didn't, so read it girl."

Candy picked up a letter opener and handed it to me. I looked into her eyes and said, "You open it."

Candy took the letter opener and began to cut away at the envelope's thick seam. My heart began to beat faster as I rested my hands on my lap. Candy cleared her throat

and began to read Derrick's heart-warming words.
Dear Shanelle,

Words cannot express how sorry I was to see you at the hospital. All I can say is that I am sorry you lost your husband. I had to write something just to let you know how I feel. It's something you taught me a long time ago. Anyway, I can only pray that you will open this letter and read it one day. Knowing you the way I do, avoiding me may be the best thing for now.

Candy connected with me by handing me the first page of the letter. My avoidance continued as I shifted my eyes to my tightly clasped hands. Her voice became softer just to compliment Derrick's refrain.

Shanelle, you have gone through so much in your life, I can't imagine any person other than you who has to once again overcome such a crazy reality. Seeing you with your son downtown that day convinced me that despite it all, you would weather the storm. If some time has passed since you opened this letter, I hope this makes sense to you because I'm going to take a risk and just say it. Do you remember our hopes and dreams for the future? My dream of becoming a doctor tested our relationship and I had to leave you behind. I realize now that there was little I could do to help you escape the past, but something deep inside of me often wonders if it's ever too late? I believe in destiny Shanelle and I know you do too. I put the poem you wrote to me in this envelope so you could remember the words you wrote to me. It hasn't been ten years, but I'm ready to see if we can finally have a meeting of the minds.

Pick up the phone Shanelle and call me.
Sincerely, after all this time,
Derrick.
(212) 333-1212

Candy pulled the poem out of the envelope. It was

folded up and resting in the corner. I snatched it from her and immediately opened the thin piece of wispy paper. A small smile cascaded across my face as Candy's face lit up with a silly grin.

"Well?" Candy asked.

"Well what?" I replied.

She sighed and said, "Call him. If you don't, I will. Damn Shanelle, you're not a mummy. See what he has to say. I'm not trying to shove him down your throat, but he still has hope, call him."

I looked at Candy like she was crazy. "Hope in what, I have a son, he doesn't want me Candy." I cleared my throat and said, "Besides, you know I promised the Fosters that I would lay low."

Candy sucked her teeth and said, "The last time I checked, the trial was over, the police aren't parked outside the door and Barbara Walters isn't trying to call your ass for an interview. It's time to take a small step forward Shanelle, just call him."

Candy toned down a bit and then finished me off. "Look, you're doing a great job with Troy, just like Alex would have wanted. But you need some adult stimulation in your life."

Honestly, there was no way I considered myself old and unavailable. All of my time with Troy replaced my need to binge on food. I was sure that once I pulled my sweatshirt off, I wouldn't mind what was underneath. Even after all these years, Derrick kept popping up but he was there for me when the chips were really down. Despite my problems, he was the only person that connected with my dreams for the future. Alex constantly boxed them up and opened it up when he was ready. But, I had to admit, if it wasn't for Alex, I wouldn't be able to afford any dreams.

Clean air began to drift downstairs from the open windows upstairs. New perspectives became my friend as

I began to inhale the crisp air around me. I stared at my folded hands and watched them open up instead of remaining closed and defensive. My own will forced me to stand up and carry my body to the phone hanging on the wall.

I grabbed the phone and the cord as Candy called out the numbers.

"212 333-1212."

My heart began to pump in hard thumps. The phone rang a total of three times before someone answered. Instead of hearing Derrick's voice, a woman answered.

"Hello."

My eyes grew wide as I contemplated hanging up. She inquired again. "Hello?"

Candy waved her hand to force me out of my trance.

"Oh, hi, hello, may I speak to Derrick please?"

She paused and said, "May I ask who's calling?"

I looked at the letter on the table and said, "This is Shanelle, returning his call."

Candy gave me the thumbs up sign, as I covered the mouthpiece. A few voices could be heard in the distance. It also sounded like a door slammed. When Derrick answered, I exhaled.

"Hello?"

"Hi Derrick, it's me, Shanelle."

Derrick exhaled too. He paused for a moment and cleared his voice. I wondered what he was thinking, but it didn't take long to find out.

"Hey, I was beginning to give up on you," Derrick said. There was relief in his voice, but I wondered if he was preoccupied.

"Did I catch you at a bad time?" I asked.

He sighed and said, "No, no, I had a study group

over, but we were just wrapping up anyway."

"Oh," was my response.

"So, I take it you just read my letter?" Derrick asked.

I held on to the phone cord and said, "It was nice, really nice."

Derrick couldn't resist riding my sentence and said, "It would be nice to see you Shanelle, it's been a long time."

I caught Candy's eye and quickly looked away.

"I wouldn't mind seeing you again, where do you want to meet?"

Derrick paused and said, "My money is kind of tight these days, so I couldn't take you to a fancy restaurant. Can you meet me in the city on Saturday night?"

I laughed and said, "You know I'm not a fancy restaurant kind of girl, let's keep it simple. How about Ray's Pizza in the Village?"

Candy nodded her head in approval as Derrick replied, "Sounds great, six o'clock?"

"Six o'clock is fine," I replied. When I hung up the phone, Candy said, "Pack a bag for you and Troy and stay at my house for the weekend, I could use the company."

I looked at her puzzled and said, "Why, aren't you doing Newark to D.C.?"

Candy laughed and said, "Clinton and I are trying to get pregnant and he is wearing my ass out girl."

I looked at her and started jumping up and down. "What! I'm going to be a Godmother?"

Candy looked at me like I was crazy and said, "Not yet, but yes, one day you will be a Godmother."

I looked her up and down and squeezed her tight. We laughed at each other's happiness like the old days, while bouts of maturity strengthened our bond.

Candy stayed with me while I packed a bag for us. She also went for the ride to pick Troy up from the Foster's house. Candy wouldn't let me out the door unless I had a cute outfit on and a full face of makeup. When Mr. Foster opened the door, he didn't recognize me at first.

"Shanelle... uh, hey, you're all dressed up, what's the occasion?"

I quickly replied, "Nothing, where's Troy?"

Candy greeted Mr. Foster and walked in behind me.

"Troy is outside with his grandmother, you're early, I thought you weren't coming until eight."

I walked towards the back door and said, "I know, I'm going to spend the weekend at Candy's and we need to get a jump on traffic."

Mr. Foster looked surprised at first, and then he smiled. "That's good," he replied. "You know you can leave Troy here if you like."

I shook my head in the middle of his sentence and said, "No, he's coming with me Pops." I knew the Fosters would take care of my little man, but I wasn't ready to leave my lifeline to Alex on any given day of the week. Having him so close to me was all the sanity I needed.

Mrs. Foster was in the back planting mums when Troy spotted me. He began running towards me screaming my name in pure delight. "Mommy mommy!" I picked him up and nuzzled in his neck. He was getting so tall and thin; it felt like I hadn't seen him in weeks.

"Wow," I exclaimed, "I think you grew some more."

Mrs. Foster got off her knees and brushed off the loose particles of dirt from her pants. She looked at my attire and immediately began her inquiry. "Hi Shanelle, hello Candy, you girls going out for a change?"

"Yeah, I'm going to Candy's house for the

weekend."

Mrs. Foster's sentiment was the same as her husband's. "Oh, Troy has extra clothes, so he'll be fine Shanelle."

I looked her in the eyes and said, "I'm taking him with me."

Her curiosity continued. "Well if you go out, who's going to watch him?"

I was annoyed at first, but it was time to take a stand in a modest way. "I'm going out mom and Candy's going to watch him."

Mrs. Foster began pulling off her gardening gloves by each finger. She looked down at the ground as if Alex was buried directly beneath her feet and said, "I see."

Candy looked at her watch and said, "We better get going Shanelle."

I stared into Mrs. Foster's eyes and smiled. I wanted her to smile back, but she didn't. I turned my back and went into the house to collect Troy's favorite toys. Mr. Foster took the initiative to change his pull up and put his jacket on as he got on his knees to hug his grandson. He grunted like an old man and said, "Troy, be good for mommy, I'll see you when you get back." Troy laughed at his silly grandpa and said, "I'll be back Pop Pop."

Tears fell down Mrs. Foster's face like we were never coming back, but I reassured her of our return. "I'll stop by and see you on Monday, ok?"

She quickly swept her tear away and said, "Okay Shanelle, see you Monday."

Derrick

It felt good going to Candy's house. They bought a four-bedroom home in Livingston, which added some much needed color to the block. Troy stayed awake for the entire drive so I was more than happy to put him down for the night once we got back to her house. Clinton was home and not flying out for two days. We nominated him as the babysitter and went to the Short Hills Mall for a mini shopping trip. Even though Alex left me well off, I was a conservative shopper. I needed a black leather jacket with boots and lucked up with a cute sale at Bloomingdales. Candy tugged at my ponytail and said, "You need to do something with that curly mop of yours before you meet Derrick."

I shook my head and said, "I know Candy, don't start."

She gave me a look and said, "When he looks at you after all this time, I want him to be blown away."

Her choice of words were emotionally damaging as I shut my eyes to prevent a vision of Alex's bloody demise on the floor of the church. Candy grabbed my wrist and said, "Oh Shanelle, I'm so sorry."

I interrupted her and said, "I know, you didn't mean it, I'm fine Candy, really." I squeezed my eyes tight and forced that memory down into a repressed cranial cavity.

The next day I kissed Troy goodbye and went to Bloomfield Center for a manicure and pedicure. After that I went to the Dominican spot on Bloomfield Avenue for a wash, clip and a doobie. I couldn't believe how long my hair was, so I made her cut it to my shoulders to shape my face. Candy finished me off with some light makeup to last me through the day.

It felt good to get dressed up. I couldn't remember the last time I put on a decent top and pants. Candy let me borrow her silver hoops and a small leather bag. I decided to drive into New York to meet Derrick so I wouldn't have to walk in new leather boots.

By the time I got to the city, I realized that Derrick and I did not speak to each other since Candy came over. I wondered if he was going to stand me up. I stood outside Ray's Pizza looking like a nervous idiot for fifteen minutes. I started getting antsy and decided to leave, but as I turned around, he was standing right in front of me smiling from ear to ear. He startled me so bad, I almost fell backwards but I caught myself as he started laughing. I looked up at him with a silly grin on my face not knowing what to say or do.

Derrick looked like he could afford more than a slice of pizza. He had a fresh shave and I could tell he just got his haircut. He didn't have on sweats or a baseball cap. He was distinctive as any New Yorker in full black attire, including a turtleneck, casual slacks and a black leather jacket. One hand was comfortably tucked in his pants pocket. His other hand was behind his back. His almond shaped eyes lit up when our eyes connected for a closer look. Derrick took the flowers he was hiding behind his back and put them on top of a mailbox right next to us. I looked down for a minute and he quickly picked my head up like he used to do in the past.

"There's nothing down there Shanelle except feet. Besides, I need a hug."

I looked into Derrick's eyes and reached up to hug him. My leather jacket was open when I embraced him. Derrick didn't reach around me on the outside of my jacket. Instead, he slid his hands underneath and wrapped his warm hands around my back in a sweet embrace. I didn't realize it at first, but he lifted me right off the ground and nuzzled his face in my hair. He inhaled at first and held his breath. When he exhaled it felt like our combined energy satisfied his soul.

"Ahh, it's so good to finally see you again Shanelle."

Having someone hold me again felt wonderful. The fact that it was someone I used to hug in the past was also comforting. When our eyes met again, all he could do was smile. He held my hand up and spun me around.

"Gorgeous as ever," he said. He took the flowers off the mailbox and handed them to me with a smile. I held the flowers up to my nose and smelled them. Derrick touched me with the tip of his finger to remove small strands of hair from my face.

"Thank you," I said ever so softly.

Derrick slid his hand into his pocket and said, "You're welcome."

I looked him up and down and said, "It doesn't look like you want pizza."

Derrick looked both ways as yellow cabs drove down the Avenue of the Americas. He quickly grabbed my hand and said, "You're right, I'm not in the mood for pizza, I just want to be with you."

We crossed the street when the coast was clear and headed towards Washington Square Park. There was a slight chill in the air, but Derrick's fast pace and warm hand kept me at a comfortable temperature. I looked up and smiled at him and he smiled back. I waited for him to speak first as we dodged the on coming traffic.

"What are you wearing Shanelle, you always smell so good."

My heels clicked along the sidewalk as I answered him. "Tresor, by Lancôme."

"I like it. It smells soft with a little bit of spunk. It's perfect for you."

I laughed and said, "I bet you say that to all the ladies." Derrick quickly shook his head and said, "The only girl in my life is called T-cell."

"A medical term?" I asked.

"Yep, I live and breath her." He looked at me with sincerity and stopped in the front of the Hagan Daz ice cream store. "Do you want some ice cream?" He asked.

"No thank you," I replied.

"You look great, I hope you're not worried about the weight thing."

I shook my head and said, "Trust me, Troy put an end to all of that."

Derrick turned to the cashier and grabbed his chocolate cone. "How are the two of you doing?" His face was filled with concern. This time he let me put my head down until I was comfortable looking at him again.

"It's day by day for me Derrick. Troy was only one when it happened so he doesn't remember much."

If it was a hot day outside, Derrick's ice cream would have melted because he was riveted by my story. I grabbed a napkin and handed it to him. I remembered how kind he was to me on the day of the shooting.

"Derrick, I never got a chance to say thank you for everything you did for me that day."

Derrick pulled me away from the counter so other people could make a purchase. He grabbed my hand and said, "Shanelle, you don't have to thank me, I'm just sorry that it happened."

Derrick watched the wind blow my hair in different directions before he spoke again.

"Let's sit in the park, is that okay with you?"

It was great being out so I said, "Sure."

There was complete darkness all around us by the time we sat down. Washington Square Park was lit up with people young and old as we sat down on a bench. Derrick turned towards me and pushed strands of hair away from my face again as I looked at him. He was making a small fuss over me but it felt nice. The conversation started with him.

"I'm glad you called me Shanelle."

"I'm glad you asked me to," I replied.

Derrick tugged on my earlobe and said, "Even though all of these people are sitting in the park, it feels like it's just me and you here."

I quietly zipped up my jacket and stared at him. I didn't have a response, but I liked what he said.

Derrick rubbed the back of my hand and said, "Are you okay Shanelle, you've been through so much..."

I silenced him by putting my finger over his mouth. I didn't want to talk about it, that was my way of coping. Instead I focused on him.

"You look great Derrick, I hope all is well in your life."

Derrick tossed his tattered napkin in the trash and looked at me with sincerity in his eyes. "Hmm," he said, "I feel like I missed alot of down time, but I'll catch up. I'm happy I stuck to my goals."

Derrick was so convincing when he spoke. Even as people walked by, there was something about him that made people stop and stare at him. His presence was so mature and genuine at the same time. I stroked his smooth face with my hand and said, "I'm so proud of you."

He held onto my hand and kissed my palm before he rested it on his lap. We stared at each other for a split second and broke out in nervous laughter. Then he asked me an interesting question.

"Do you think we really had a chance back then Shanelle?"

I immediately answered, "No, we didn't."

His face became serious this time. "How about now?" he asked.

"Why me?" I asked.

Derrick sucked his teeth like I was supposed to know the answer. "I don't know, Shanelle, it just feels like I need to take a chance." Derrick pulled me off the bench and wrapped his arms around me. I laid my head on his chest and closed my eyes. His heart was beating fast as he continued to rub my back.

Derrick nuzzled his mouth next to my ear and said, "It feels good to hold you again Shanelle."

Trust me, I enjoyed the hug, but I wasn't sure if Derrick was saying the same thing to other women. I wasn't looking for any drama after all this time. I looked at him and asked, "Derrick, do you have a girlfriend?"

He sat down on the park bench and pulled me into his frame. He rubbed my hand with his thumb and said, "Shanelle, I had a girlfriend but it didn't work out. It's hard trying to find a genuine woman like you. I think they're all lined up waiting for that MD to get behind my name, but I'm not having it."

"You're right," I said, "You worked hard for that, you need a real woman by your side to support you."

"Like you?" he asked.

His question caught me off gaurd so I laughed, not knowing what to say.

Derrick relaxed his shoulders and said, "Real woman like you; tough and not afraid to follow a dream."

My face frowned when he mentioned the dream part. "Derrick, you know what's been going on in my life, I didn't follow my dreams, I followed someone else's."

Derrick squeezed my hand and said, "You mean Alex?"

I blinked once and said, "Yes, Alex. In my crazy mixed up world, I ran to him and gave him everything he wanted, especially a son."

"And you're a good mother," Derrick said, "Is it too late to follow your dreams, your only twenty-one… well make that twenty-two, next week right?"

I smiled, happy that he remembered. "Yes," I said, "I'll be twenty-two."

Derrick threw his hands in the air and said, "Well, what's the problem? Go back to school, you have your whole life ahead of you Shanelle."

I started to yawn and said, "You're right."

Derrick grabbed my chin and said, "You look sleepy, are you tired?"

I perked up, not wanting to leave him and said, "I can hang for another hour or two."

"Good!" Derrick replied. "I don't want you to leave, but I know Troy probably misses you."

I smiled at his concern for my son and said, "Candy's watching him for me, so he's in good hands."

Derrick smacked my leg and said, "Good then, let's go to the Blue Note."

I looked down at my throbbing feet and wondered if I could make it there by foot. Derrick looked down and said, "You had to be cute and buy those new boots?"

I put my feet up on the bench. Derrick zipped my boots down and said, "Take them off, I'll give you a piggy back ride."

I grabbed Derrick's wrist and said, "You're crazy!" Derrick snatched my boots off and said, "I'm a medical student and I don't give a damn. Besides, this is New York, anything goes, even a piggy back ride."

Derrick stood up and turned around. I climbed on his back, flowers in hand and a smile on my face. Derrick carried my boots and walked all the way to the Blue Note as passerbys happily strolled along. When we got there, we took a seat in the back. Derrick propped my legs on top of his under the table and began to massage my feet. A local artist was playing the saxophone as we quietly stared at each other. Derrick ordered a drink while I sipped on spring water. He grabbed my left hand and stroked each of my fingers. Then he looked at my ring finger and smiled. He leaned over and whispered in my ear, "Are you sure you're doing okay?" I looked at my ring and said, "I miss him."

Derrick continued to massage my feet and said, "It takes time Shanelle, just take it day by day." He pulled my chair closer to him and I put my head on his shoulder. We ordered dinner and listened to the music. Derrick had nothing else to do but stare at me as I enjoyed my foot massage. Nothing else needed to be said between us. Even if Derrick wanted me back, that was going to take time too. We were both the same in many ways, but time had changed us. I looked back at Derrick and smiled. He picked up his drink with his eyes gazing at me. We excused each other to wash our hands before dinner came. Comedy came to us in the form of feet and food not mixing well. When the laughter settled to silence, I wondered what he was thinking, but I didn't ask. He looked at his watch and patted my lap.

Thirty minutes passed as the waiter brought us our dinner. We shared small talk and shared our food like old times. It felt good being with him and talking about medical school. I was glad we were catching up, but there was little about my life that I wanted to share with the exception of Troy.

The clock forced our priorities to float to the surface while I went to the payphone to check on Troy. Derrick paid the bill and picked up our jackets from the coat stand. I went to use the ladies room and he was graciously waiting outside when I stepped out.

Derrick quietly helped me into my jacket and led me to the exit. Once outside, he switched positions with me to shield me from the street. Derrick softly grabbed my hand and said, "I've got to hit the books tonight, but I want you to know I had a nice time."

"Me too," I replied.

Derrick tugged on my earlobe and said, "I'd like to see you again Shanelle, if you don't mind."

I took a small piece of paper out of my pocketbook and wrote my phone number down including Candy's number. I looked at his pant pocket and tucked it inside. He smiled at me and said, "Look at us all grown up now."

"How about that," I replied.

Derrick licked his lips and said, "Tell me what's in that head of yours Shanelle?" Derrick asked.

I looked down the street and thought about what I would say to him. The wind blew my hair into my face as Derrick softly swept it behind my ears.

My response was short and to the point. "Derrick, I don't know what to think so far. There's so much time between us I guess I'm afraid of getting hurt."

Derrick grabbed my chin and said, "Shanelle, I couldn't do that to you, it's not in me."

I wanted to believe him, but it was hard. He seemed so perfect and I was struggling with the idea of a new commitment.

"Derrick, you can have any girl you want, I mean any woman you want. Why me?" I asked.

Derrick sighed and said, "How about this, let's not

try to figure out all this stuff right now. Let me prove how much I care for you first. I think everything else will fall into place. Besides, it's your turn to figure out what you want."

Derrick began to organize his own thoughts and said, "Think about it Shanelle, if you go back to school while I start my residency, we're going to be busy. In order for me to be a competent doctor, I need to be three steps ahead of myself. I don't have time to be out there chasing skirts." He paused to strengthen the intensity in his statement. "Trust me, I'm not interested in chasing skirts. But you might get a little frustrated if I'm not able to spend enough time with you. If there are any breaks in between, I would really like to reacquaint myself with you again."

I was concerned about one more thing, so I quickly asked, "What about Troy?"

Derrick laughed and said, "How could I resist him? It'll be a good excuse to act like a kid again."

Derrick changed his expression like a light bulb went off in his head. "Listen, if you're going to be around, meet me for dinner at my mom's house tomorrow." He changed his expression again and said, "Bring Troy, I would love to see him and so would my mother."

There was trust in his eyes, so I quickly said yes as we headed back to Ninth Street. When we reached the car, I took my car keys out of my pocket and offered him a ride back to his apartment. He refused and said, "No, I want you to get back on the road, it's getting late."

I put my pocket book on my shoulder and leaned up against the Jeep. Derrick looked me up and down with his almond shaped eyes. My lips puckered to the side because I knew he wanted to ask me for a kiss.

"Before I let you go, can I…" He didn't finish his sentence so I started laughing at the handsome jokester.

"Can you what?" I replied.

Derrick leaned over and put his lips next to my ear.
"Can I squeeze your nose, it's so irresistible."

I laughed out loud and said, "If that's all you want,
sure, go ahead and squeeze my nose Derrick."

Derrick grabbed me by my waist and said, "Sike! I
really want to do this…"

Derrick put his lips on top of mine and slid his
tongue into my mouth. The drink he had at the Blue Note
was sweet and sour which riddled my taste buds and made
my nipples get hard underneath my leather jacket. Derrick
pulled me in closer and forced his tongue further into my
mouth as he began to moan. I don't think it mattered who
was walking down the street because we were focused on
our moment. I pulled away from him for a minute and
looked up at him. Derrick swept my lips with his thumb
and said, "What's wrong?"

I grabbed his face with my hands and said,
"Nothing, kiss me again."

Derrick obliged and caressed me with his hands
while he slowly explored my mouth with his tongue. He
took his hand and traced the small of my back with three
fingers just below the waist of my jeans. It was a new and
wonderful feeling that I had yet to experience. I didn't
want him to stop, but he did with a long sigh.

"Okay, I've got to go and so do you. Will you come
for dinner tomorrow?"

I looked up at him and said, "What time?"

"Around five, come casual so we can wrestle."

I put my hand on my hip and said, "And what
about your mother and Troy?"

Derrick laughed and said, "My mom has some old
Sesame Street footage on video. We'll send them upstairs
after dinner. She won't mind."

I didn't have a chance to answer because Derrick

started kissing me again. When he stopped, he grabbed my car keys and opened the door. I took my jacket off before I got in while Derrick watched my every move. I started up the car and rolled down the window. Derrick finally squeezed my nose and said, "Remember Shanelle, it's your turn. I'll see you tomorrow."

Besides the pleasurable feeling between my legs, deep down inside, it was the first time in a long time I felt good. I looked in the rear view mirror and smiled at myself as Derrick hailed a taxi. I smoothed the remaining lipstick across my lips and turned on the radio for the ride home.

By the time I got back to Candy's house, Troy was still up and bouncing around. Candy was smart enough to give him a bath and put his pajamas on while they sat on the couch and listened to mommy's first date. I plopped next to Candy while Troy climbed in my lap. Before I talked about the date, I gave Candy something to think about and said, "I think I'm going to attend late registration at St. James, what do you think?'

Candy hugged me and said, "Sounds like a plan, you can stay here if you want, there's enough room." I laughed at first and said, "Oh no, I know there's too much bumping and grinding going on in here. Troy and I will get an apartment, but you can help me out and watch Troy while I go to class."

Candy playfully poked Troy in the stomach and said, "Girl, the Fosters are gonna have a fit if you come back here."

I nodded my head in agreement and said, "Candy, I can't let anyone decide for me anymore, it's my turn, you know what I mean?"

Candy gave me a high five and said, "Girl, do your thang! Alex left you straight and you would be crazy not to go back to school."

I gave Candy a high five and said, "Oh yeah, Derrick asked me to come to his mother's house for dinner and he wants me to bring Troy."

Before Candy could answer, Troy stood up on the couch and clapped his hands. He was getting sleepy so we headed upstairs to the guest room with Candy in tow.

"Are you going to bring him?" Candy asked.

"Of course, wherever I go, he goes."

The three of us climbed into bed. Troy quickly fell asleep underneath me while Candy and I decided to talk.

"So tell me about Dr. Derrick."

I put my hands under my head and said, "He's the same in some ways, but different in other ways. One nice thing about Derrick is that he likes to be out. With Alex, we were always huddled in the house like Alex wanted to escape from the world. Derrick seems like he wants to enjoy the world around him. I guess being cooped up in a library all day makes him stir crazy."

By the time I finished my sentence, Candy was fast asleep. She didn't know if she was pregnant yet, but she was sleeping anytime the opportunity came. Having Troy all day must have also worn her out. I put a blanket across the two of them and quickly took out my journal. Nothing meant more to me than three simple words. I wrote the words slowly and carefully before a poem became me.

Take your time

Abundance on earth,
Wrought with guilt and pleasure,
Time can only measure
My intensity
Intertwined with my passion for life.
So much of what rests within me
Cultivates our child.
Each grain of sand
Sweeps in various directions
Some of which I cannot control
While some embeds in my conscious and
Rests with my soul.
Strong conviction,
Stand tall,
Loving thyself first
Sharing with others
I finally behold,
An innate constitution to survive
This crazy test of time
Please stand back
As I claim what is rightfully mine...
Self love.

I put my pen and paper down and walked into the guest bathroom. There in the mirror, a reflection of Alex came to me in my thoughts. I closed my eyes to feel him as a warm sensation flowed through my body. A cool breeze from the window caressed my face and whispered to me that everything was going to be ok. I opened my eyes and looked at the reflection of myself. There was clarity and calm. No voices entered my head and taunted me. I began to sing an old song and thought about seeing Derrick and his mother again. I also thought about staying an extra night at Candy's house so I could go to St. James for late registration. If Candy couldn't watch Troy, at least I had his stroller to get him around the campus. I took a deep breath and sighed. For once in my life, the things I decided to do on my own felt free and easy. Derrick was right, it was "my turn."

I kept Troy on a tight schedule Sunday afternoon so he wouldn't be a crank pot at dinner. He was teething a-lot so I decided to give him some Motrin before we left.

Candy wasn't happy with my fashion choice or Troy's comfortable Gap sweat suit. I wanted to have fun for a change and I knew Troy was up for the challenge. By the time we reached his mother's house, I could smell dinner from the walkway. The September foliage and her comfy house brought back memories of the refuge Derrick provided me in the past. I made a checklist in my mind to stay an extra day to give Mrs. Viv a visit and speak my peace.

Derrick opened the door before I rang the doorbell. Troy walked in like he was the mayor and the local plumber. He had a complete fixation with tools and was dying to fix anything broken in Ms. Johnson's home. Ms. Johnson immediately wiped her hands on her apron and gave me a warm hug. "It's so good to see you again Shanelle, make yourself at home."

By the looks of things, it was easy to do. Derrick took Troy on a tour of the house, banging on anything that looked broken. Ms. Johnson laughed and said, "Derrick was the same way at that age, I think boys are programmed for tools."

Derrick laid across the living room floor when they came downstairs and let Troy bang on his "broken heart." Troy laughed hysterically while Derrick jerked his body up and down every time Troy hit him. I was glad he was spending time with him because I didn't do those things with him at home. We were always reading or coloring our time away. I got up to offer my help to Ms. Johnson, but Derrick pulled me down to the ground like a little kid.

"Derrick, stop!" I said. It had little effect as Troy jumped on his head and started smacking him. Derrick grabbed us both and started tickling us as Ms. Johnson peeked in and smiled at us romping on the floor. Troy managed to break free and Derrick slipped me a quick kiss when he wasn't looking and said, "I missed you, did you miss me?" I pondered the thought and said, "Hmm, a little."

I stood up and made Troy sit down before we ate. Ms. Johnson took him to the bathroom to wash his hands. Derrick took the opportunity to snuggle up next to me while a few thoughts popped in my head.

"So, Derrick, you don't have a girlfriend?"

'No," he replied, "Do you have a boyfriend?"

I smacked his leg and said, "You know I don't have a boyfriend, stop playing. The only boy in my life is my son." We looked up and they were coming down the stairs hand and hand.

"I hope you don't mind Shanelle, but he asked to sit on the potty, so I took Derrick's old potty seat out and dusted it off."

I started laughing hysterically and said, "You still have his potty?"

Ms. Johnson looked at Derrick and said, "Go upstairs and see for yourself."

Derrick pulled me off the couch and said, "Thanks mom, last time I checked I was a grown man."

I smacked Derrick's shoulder and said, "More like a mama's boy." We headed upstairs and Derrick pulled me past the bathroom and into his old room. Everything was still in tact from his glory days in high school. I began to look around while Derrick sat on his bed smiling at me. I started laughing because his bed looked so small. Derrick pulled me on his lap and said, "My poor bed, I couldn't get lucky with you back then for nothing."

I punched him in his arm and said, "I'm still worth the wait."

Derrick nodded his head in agreement and pulled me on top of him. He started smiling and said, "Why do I feel so comfortable with you?"

I sat up and said, "I guess we just vibe well together." Derrick shook his head and said, "No, I think you're the only girl who really understands me." I put my hand on my heart and said, "Why Derrick, I'm so honored."

Derrick started to rub my back and said, "Hmm, I want you to be naughty."

I bit my lip and said, "We better go downstairs before your mother sends Troy after us."

Just as I suspected, Ms. Johnson and Troy were at the bottom of the stairs waiting for us to eat. Before we ate, we held hands and said our grace. Derrick squeezed my hands and kicked me under the table. It felt good having someone I could be silly with instead of being so serious all the time. Ms. Johnson made Troy's plate while my son picked and prodded at his table napkin.

Troy loved to sing while he ate his food so Ms. Johnson laughed the whole meal. Derrick looked happy until the doorbell rang. Ms. Johnson's eyes shifted quickly to Derrick as she got up to answer the door. I could her a young woman in the background greeting Ms. Johnson as Derrick got up and excused himself. He wiped his mouth and said, "Excuse me Shanelle."

Before Derrick could get out of the dining room, a pretty woman stepped into the room with a box in her hand. She looked at me, then Troy before she turned to Derrick. She handed him a box and said, "Playing house?"

Derrick took the box from her hands and placed it on the floor. Ms. Johnson came back to the table with an irritated look on her face. Derrick pointed to me and said, "Bridgette, this is…"

She held her hand up and said, "You must be Shanelle."

Derrick grabbed her wrist and said, "Yes, this is Shanelle, if you let me finish. This is her son Troy." Troy mumbled with a mouth full of food, "Hi lady."

Ms. Johnson was tickled pink. Whoever she was, you could tell she wasn't welcome in her house. I quickly looked her up and down and immediately thought of Derrick's need to have a trophy girl. She looked at Derrick and pointed to the box. "Take care Rick and good luck." She kissed Ms. Johnson on her cheek, but it wasn't well received. Ms. Johnson rolled her eyes in her head and said, "Bye Bridgette, take care." Derrick led her out of the dining room and to her car. We could see them through the window as Ms. Johnson patted the corners of her lips with her napkin. She looked at me and said, "Lord forgive me but I can't stand that girl." After that she smiled and said, "Now that she saw you, I guess that's the last I'll see of her."

I looked out the window and looked at her car. I

immediately thought of the girl he was with at Mueller's just before Candy's wedding. My defenses went up in an instant as I looked at my watch. I stood up and started cleaning up. Troy began to pout when I took his half finished plate away. The more time Derrick spent outside with her, the more stupid I felt.

Ms. Johnson grabbed my wrist and said, "Shanelle, she's an old girlfriend trying to hang on. Derrick dumped her six months ago." She squeezed my wrist tighter and said, "Don't runaway because of Ms. Pris."

I looked at Troy grabbing the serving spoon from the macaroni and cheese. He was still hungry and trying to force the spoon into his mouth. Ms. Johnson took the spoon from him and started laughing. "Girl, this boy reminds me of Derrick the way he eats. God bless him, he can sure put away some food."

My eyes shifted back to the window, but the car was long gone. When I looked up Derrick was standing in the entrance. Ms. Johnson didn't say a word as Derrick asked me to step outside. The only thing I felt connected to was Troy so I said, "Mommy will be right back."

Funny, Troy was so engrossed in Ms. Johnson's food, he didn't give a rat's ass where I went. My defenses immediately kicked in the moment I stepped outside. I folded my hands across my chest.

Derrick looked at me and said, "C'mon Shanelle, you know I've been straight up with you."

"I'm not trying to be your rebound girl you know, I've been through too much and I'm not havin' it Derrick."

Derrick grabbed my shoulders and said, "Shanelle, we broke up a long time ago, I know what I want and that's you." I turned around and looked at Derrick's house. Thoughts of Troy quickly came to focus.

"Derrick, I've got alot going on, including my son. So it's not just me to think about. I've got to think about him every waking moment of the day, so if you want to be with me, Troy has to fit right in too."

Derrick took my hand and started walking down the front path to the sidewalk. "Look Shanelle," Derrick said. "My life is straight as this sidewalk, graduate from Cornell, four year residency at University and right into pediatric medicine." He cleared his throat and said, "Has anything stopped me yet?"

"No, nothing at all." I replied.

Derrick folded his hands across his chest and said, "Now, do you think I have time for nonsense with the life I mapped out for myself?" He dropped his hands at his sides while sincerity rested in his eyes. I got smart with him and said, "No, you look about as serious as a heart attack."

"Don't play with me Shanelle," Derrick replied.

"Okay, okay, I'm sorry," I said. "But what do you want from me?"

Derrick relaxed his shoulders and said, "Shanelle, just be you, I don't want a machine, a toy or somebody to lie to me just to make me feel good." He rested his hands on my shoulders and said, "I think if we do that everything will just fall into place, I know it, I can feel it."

A cool breeze whipped through me as I looked up into the sky. The moon was so bright I was immediately drawn to the beauty of it all.

Derrick grabbed my hand and said, "Tell me Shanelle, is it too much for you right now?"

I knew he was referring to Alex and I was grateful for his concern. I took a deep breath and squeezed his hand.

"No, I like your plan, a simple course with the opportunity for dips and curves along the way, that's cool."

"Well then," Derrick replied, "Let's go back in the house and finish dinner, I'm up for the challenge."

By the time we went back inside, Troy was finished for the night, fast asleep in Ms. Johnson's arms on the living room couch. Just like Derrick predicted, she put an old Sesame Street video in the VCR. Derrick put his arm around me and smiled at the two of them. He looked at me and said, "Do you still have the Kermit doll I gave you?" I looked up at him and said, "I think it's at Candy's parent's house in the attic."

My mind quickly shifted to Alex and the big teddy bear he gave me when we started dating. Derrick sighed and said, "Well, I'm going to have to do something about that."

Derrick and I went into the kitchen and cleaned everything in sight. He hadn't changed a bit and he was happy to see that I was still neat and orderly. After we straightened up the dining room, we sat down and shared a cup of ice cream. He fed me a spoonful as I began to talk about school.

"I'm going to register at St. James tomorrow."

Derrick looked surprised and said, "That's great, how many credits?"

I smiled and said, "You know me, eighteen of course."

Derrick replied, "Who's going to watch Troy?"

I put a scoop of ice cream in his mouth and said, "First I have to see what classes are available and then I'll work something out with Candy."

Derrick put his spoon down and said, "Can I make a suggestion?"

"Sure," I replied.

"Well, my mother retired six months ago and she could really use some company during the day. Besides, you can drop him off here and walk to St. James."

The offer was tempting, but I wanted to run it by Candy first. I looked at Derrick and said, "Let me talk to

Candy about it first.

Derrick looked surprised at first and said, "Okay Shanelle." He stood up and put the empty dish in the sink. I walked up behind him and placed my hands around his waist. He turned around and hugged me back.

"What was that for?" he asked.

"Thanks for listening, I'm excited about going back to school."

"Good" Derrick said, "And you should let my mother watch Troy while you take St. James by storm." Derrick kissed me on my forehead and said, "I'll admit, if you do that, I'll be able to keep up with you."

I looked up at him and said, "Well, I'm glad you're looking out for me, but I'm a big girl now."

Derrick wasn't hearing too much of that and said, "Okay, I'll give you that, but a little help here or there won't kill you, I'm only trying to help."

I looked at the clock and decided that it was time to go. Derrick agreed because he needed to do some research.

He picked Troy up from his mother's sleeping arms and wrestled his arms into his jacket. He looked awkward doing it, but I didn't mind him taking the initiative. I thanked Ms. Johnson for a wonderful dinner and she in turn thanked me for my courtesies. "Shanelle," she said. "I remember when I met you at Livingston Mall, you were so sweet and you still are. In fact, you remind me of myself when I was your age."

Derrick tapped his mother's shoulders and said, "C'mon mom, don't start going down memory lane on us, Troy needs to go to bed."

Ms. Johnson gave me a wink and said, "Goodnight, take care of that sweet boy of yours." She bent down to say goodnight to Troy as he planted a sleepy wet kiss on her cheek that melted her heart away.

"Shanelle, it was lovely having the two of you over, I hope we can do this again." She kissed me on the cheek again and headed upstairs. It was a nice feeling knowing that both of them cared about me.

Derrick carried Troy to the car and put him in his car seat. My little man was so worn out, he went right back to sleep in an instant. Derrick grabbed my hand and said, "I'll call you tonight once I get back to the city."

I kissed him on the cheek and said, "Okay, you do that." I turned to get in the car, but his schoolboy charm stopped me as he grabbed my hand. He held it next to his heart and said, "Dance with me."

I started shaking my head as he swirled me around on the sidewalk and pulled me into his body again. Derrick serenaded me on the street as we stared at Troy. A few horns honked at our graceful dance as we reacted with soft laughter. There was no way I could go wrong in his arms. Derrick was an emotional anchor, but I still felt free to do whatever I wanted. I reached up and grabbed him around the neck as he picked me up and spun me around. We were catching up on old times, but moving forward in the right direction. After a long kiss goodnight, Derrick slammed the door as I pulled off down the street.

Back to School

The next day, with Candy and Troy at my side, we went to St. James for late registration. My transcript placed me in my junior year and I only needed thirty credits to graduate. After looking at the course schedule, we agreed that I would go to school three days a week while she looked after Troy. Derrick's suggestion was nice, but I was cautious about being too close to him.

Going to the Bursar' office to pay my bill was the highlight of my day. I whispered thank you to Alex for his generosity. Because of him, I could afford school and provide an even better life for our son. In my heart of hearts, I knew Alex would be proud of me.

When we walked out of the building, early fall foliage fell from the trees in the form of yellow and red leaves. It was Alex's favorite time of year as hints of nature's pleasure feathered down in front of my face and landed on the ground. I smiled as I looked into the sky happily holding Troy's hand. I think Candy sensed my sentiment because she smiled at me and said, "It's a beautiful day Shanelle, I'm proud of you." She grabbed Troy's hand as we walked back to my car.

During the ride back to Candy's house, I looked at people along South Harrison Street and wondered who besides me, felt free. The time I spent at home taking care of Alex and Troy forced me into a strange abyss. Deep in my heart, I wanted a way out, but I didn't have the courage to clear a path. Having Troy sculpted me into motherhood regardless of preparation. Despite everything, I still managed to smile. I had a lot to be thankful for as the needy walked up to my window for change. I dropped fifty cents in his hand and stayed focus. Belief in myself guided my belief in others. In retrospect, I think Alex would have gained more out of life with that motto instead of defining his redemption. Layers of doubt began to peel away as I turned up the radio and bobbed my head to a new beat called freedom.

By the time we reached Candy's house, Candy and Troy were cranky and wiped out from the back to school experience. They headed upstairs for a nap and I went to Joyce Leslie's to pick up some outfits for school. On the way home, stopping at Mrs. Viv's house was a must. I needed to bury some old issues.

Mrs. Viv was out front, tending to her wilted garden. A "House for Sale" sign was mounted on the front lawn while she dug into the dry dirt. There was no sign of Kiko or Steven. She heard my footsteps and abruptly turned around.

"Shanelle," she said, in a surprised tone.

"Hello Vivian," I replied.

She quickly smoothed her clothes out and began to chuckle to herself. "So, I'm no longer mom, momma or mommy, just Vivian huh?"

Before I could answer, she scoured me over from head to toe and said, "I take it your father told you what happened?"

The sight of falling shingles from the roof offered a humble distraction to our dilemma.

"Yeah, he told me."

A symbol of my half blood landed as a black crow positioned himself on the gutter.

"Where's Steven?" I asked, as I looked at the smeared windows.

Mrs. Viv's hands folded across her chest in defense mode. "It was too much for me all alone, so I had to put him in long term care."

The sadness in her eyes was so deep, she looked like she was a million miles away. Compassion for my son slowly rose to the surface. She looked me in the eyes and said, "How's Troy, he's, let's see, he's two now right?"

I shook my head and smiled for my healthy son. "Yes, he's two years old."

Then she went into classic attack mode, envious of my outward stability. "That boy is going to need a father Shanelle."

Her comment was true, but her opinion meant little.

I mumbled under my breath, "Yeah, you're one to know."

"What did you say?" Mrs. Viv asked.

I ignored her and said, "What's the asking price for the house?" She looked at me and said, "I'm not going to get much for it because it needs so much work."

"*A house of horrors, I bet it does,*" I thought. I scratched my arm and said, "Any idea where you're going to move to?" I asked.

"South," she replied.

Realizing that this was possibly our final farewell, I looked her in the eyes and said, "Well, let me get out of here, take care Vivian," I said.

She waved her hand up in the air and plopped back into the dirt like I never existed. The mums she stuck in the ground didn't have a fighting chance as she beat a circular dust cloud into the earth. I started up the car, thrilled at the fact that someone else gave birth to me.

By the time I got back to Candy's house, Clinton was home and Troy was sprawled across the floor playing with some new blocks he bought for him. They were spoiling him rotten, but for the moment, it didn't matter because it made me feel like he had lots of family around him. When I opened the door, Troy jumped up and scrambled into my arms. He kissed my face and exclaimed, "Mommy! Mommy! Mommy!" I kissed him back and said, "Mommy missed you too sweetie."

Candy was fast asleep in Clinton's arms, which tickled me to death. The smile on his face suggested that there was good news to be told but he didn't offer any information. I smiled to myself because I knew Candy was going to tell me one way or another.

I packed a small bag and chatted with Clinton before my long ride home to Brick. A pit stop at the Fosters was a must. I needed to tell them about school. I knew they were going to be devastated, but I had every intention of letting them see Troy, especially during the weekend. Just before I walked out the door, Derrick called, anxious to hear the news about school.

"Hey, how did it go? I didn't hear from you all day."

I was glad to be so busy and taking charge. "It went great, I'm registered, classes start tomorrow."

"You sound happy Shanelle," Derrick said.

"I do?" I asked.

"Yeah, I can hear it in your voice, I'm happy for you."

While Derrick was focused on the sound of my happiness, I began to focus on the mature base in his voice.

"When can I see you again?" I asked.

Derrick remained poised and said, "Here in New York?"

"No silly, come to South Jersey this weekend. We can take Troy to the beach and then have dinner."

Derrick seemed surprised.

"What?" I asked and then continued, "Did I say something wrong?"

"No, I just thought that…" Derrick immediately cut his sentence off as silence erupted in the background.

I quickly cut him off and said, "I'd like to see you, is there any harm in that request?"

Derrick replied, "No, that's fine."

It was just that easy. We made plans for a day at the beach and dinner. I decided that Troy would go to the Fosters so I could spend some time with Derrick.

The Fosters were surprised to finally see Troy and I, but like I predicted, they weren't happy to hear me contemplate my change of life.

Mr. Foster buried his head in his hands as he sat on the couch and said, "Sell the house, why do you want to do that?"

I stood up as they watched me make my speech across the floor. "I'm going to buy my parent's house in North Orange, gut the whole thing out and put an addition on it." I looked at Mr. Foster with his years of knowledge and said, "There will be plenty of room for you when you visit us."

Mr. Foster couldn't part his lips so I continued. "I'll use the proceeds from me and Alex's…" I paused for a minute. Saying his name was strange, but I continued my quest for freedom. "I'll use the proceeds from the sale of the house for Troy's education, maybe he can go to St. James Prep one day."

My pride for North Orange did not sit well with them. Mrs. Foster said, "Shanelle, Alex used to tell me that North Orange is not a safe neighborhood."

I stood defiantly and said, "Well, that's where my

hcart is telling me to go and I want to complete two degree programs at St. James. It's five minutes away and that's that."

A tear rolled down Mrs. Foster's face as she stared at Troy. I met her needs first.

"Troy can come for long weekends, I'm not going to keep him away, you're his family."

Mrs. Foster looked desperately into my eyes and said, "What about Thanksgiving and Christmas?"

I stroked her face and said, "Especially Thanksgiving and Christmas, you think this boy wants to miss your fried turkey?"

Troy perked up and said, "Nana, I'm hungry!"

It was all Mrs. Foster needed to hear as she grabbed Troy's hand and led him into the kitchen.

Mr. Foster put his hand on my shoulder and made me sit down. He looked into my eyes and said, "Shanelle, now I know you're ready to handle everything and that's fine. But I just want you to rethink the house thing. Money is not an issue for you and you know that. Why don't you hold on to the house, it's close to the shore and you can use it as a second home in the summer. Trust me, you'll want to get to the beach when the weather gets warm." He squeezed my hand and said, "You know how much Alex loved the beach, don't you want Troy to have that love too?"

Mr. Foster was right on the money as I shook my head up and down. A warm sensation flowed throughout my body and awakened my senses. I looked at Mr. Foster and said, "You know you have to take Troy fishing too."

Before Mr. Foster answered, Troy and Mrs. Foster were heading back into the living room. I looked at the two of them and said, "I'll keep the house as long as you look after it for me while I'm gone."

The Fosters responded immediately and said, "Sure

Shanelle, we will." I hugged them both and said, "I'm having company Saturday, can you watch Troy for me in the evening?"

They looked shocked, but Mr. Foster accepted change first and said, "No problem Shanelle, Troy can come here anytime, day or night."

A quick hug completed my stay as I headed for the door. Mrs. Foster looked sad, but the strength in Mr. Foster was the foundation she needed.

By the time Saturday came, I was exhausted. I completed three days of classes, unlimited playtime with Troy and a long ride back home to Brick on Friday night. I was so busy with everything, Derrick and I barely talked but he called me Friday evening to confirm our date.

"I'll be there in the morning," he said.

I wanted him to feel comfortable staying at the house, so I asked him how he felt about our plans for the weekend.

"That's fine Shanelle, as long as you're comfortable."

I grabbed the phone cord and said, "I'm comfortable and I miss you Derrick."

He sighed out loud and said, "I miss you too Shanelle."

We said goodbye and I gently placed the phone down on the receiver. Troy was off in the distance singing to himself, happy to be home. His side profile was the spitting image of his father. As I watched him bop up and down, I sat on the couch and continued to watch him. Thoughts of Derrick began to consume me. I was longing for his affection and company. I loved Derrick's free spirit attitude. It was like a breath of fresh air and before I could blink an eye, he was at the door with a snorkel sticking out of his mouth. When we opened the door for him, Troy immediately started laughing. He pointed at him as I said,

"Look at him Troy he's so silly."

Troy raised his hand and said, "Hi, Mr. Dee."

Derrick held his hands up like a monster and roared in silence like he was the creature from the black lagoon. He chased Troy into the kitchen while I ran upstairs to grab some bags and returned to find the two of them rough housing on the floor. Troy was pounding him on his chest and laughing like a little version of Alex. Derrick settled him down and said, "Are we ready?"

Troy grabbed his Bert and Ernie beach towel and said, "Ready Mr. Dee!"

We marched out to the car and packed the trunk as my neighbor smiled at me. Even the look on her face suggested that it was time to move on with my life. We drove to Point Pleasant for a quiet day on the beach as Troy and Derrick frolicked in the sand. Troy was growing by leaps and bounds as I stared at the two of them. They played Frisbee and tag as I watched Derrick run up and down. After a full forty minutes of horseplay, Troy ate a snack and finally drifted off to sleep. Derrick took the opportunity to snuggle next to me.

"Can I share that beach chair with you?" he asked.

It was a breezy September day, but cool enough to snuggle, so I stood up and let him sit in it first, before I plopped between his legs. I turned around, looked at him and said, "Hello again."

Derrick grabbed my face and kissed me as my body began to melt. He paused for a minute and wiped my lips with his thumb. "You taste so good Shanelle."

I teased him and said, "I just kissed you the other day, did you forget?" He shook his head and said, "No, I missed you and you're starting to taste more mature."

Derrick massaged the side of my thigh as I turned around to face the ocean. He buried his neck into mine and began to whisper in my ears as my nipples became aroused. Foreplay took place right on the beach while he nibbled on my earlobe and told me how much he missed me. Kitty began to wake up after a long hiatus and the lion in his pants began to stir. We giggled under our breath and shared slices of a sweet tangerine while Derrick kissed my neck. He started laughing to himself so I turned around to see what was so funny.

"What?" I asked.

"Nothing," he said, "I want to ask you a question, but I don't want you to laugh."

"I won't laugh, what is it?" I asked.

"Will you be my girlfriend?" he asked.

I pressed my nose up against his face and said, "Now this is a flashback Derrick, where's my ring so we can go steady."

Without hesitation, he took off his college ring and slipped it on my finger next to my wedding ring. He looked down at my left hand and said, "Houston, we have a problem." I looked at my left hand, slid my rings off and put it on my right hand. We looked into each other's eyes and shared a long kiss under the warm sun. Troy began to wrestle himself from his nap and immediately began to stretch.

"Hey big man, how was your nap?" Derrick asked.

I moved out the way so Derrick could get up.

"Can you take him to the bathroom to pee, he's just getting the hang of the whole potty thing." Derrick hoisted Troy on his shoulders and said, "No problem, we can handle it."

I watched them walk away as seagulls flew above me in the distance. It was strange watching my late husband's son being whisked away by my old love. I looked at the ocean to settle my feelings and appreciate the love that Alex had for me. It felt good being with Derrick again and I was willing to take a chance with him.

Needless to say, Troy adored him. Whatever the outcome, I felt like a new person, ready and willing to take on the challenge.

We quickly wrapped up our day at the beach to drop Troy off at the Foster's house. Derrick knew where we were going and I think he felt a little nervous. I didn't want to hide our relationship anymore, so hand in hand, we walked up to the door with Troy in tow. Troy started banging on the door for his grandparents.

"Nana! Pop Pop, open the door." For a two year old, he was picking up speed in the language department. Derrick and I smiled at each other as Derrick nervously adjusted Troy's overnight bag on his shoulder. The door opened with disbelief, then surprise.

"Shanelle," Mrs. Foster said, "You're early."

"I know," I said, "But I didn't want to keep him in the sun all day." I paused and then said, "Mom, this is Derrick, uh… Derrick Johnson."

Troy started pulling Derrick into the house exclaiming, "C'mon Mr. Dee!"

Mr. Foster came into the living room wiping his hands off from his barbecue. Troy ran up to him and said, "Pop Pop, that's Mr. Dee."

Troy pointed at Derrick as he walked up to him and extended his hand. Mr. Foster looked like he needed the company.

"Nice to meet you Mr. Dee, care for a beer?"

Derrick's shoulders relaxed as he shook his head laughing, "Sure, thanks for the offer." The three of them headed out back while Mrs. Foster stared in disbelief. She came out of her trance and said, "He looks familiar." I smiled softly and said, "He was at the funeral."

"Oh," she replied.

I looked at her and said, "I hope you're not upset that I brought him over early?"

Mrs. Foster looked back at Alex's picture on the wall and said, "No honey, I understand."

Laughter graced our ears as we looked out the window. From the looks of things, Derrick was a shoe-in with Mr. Foster. He was pointing at the joints in his body while Derrick nodded his head up and down.

"Lord, what is he doing?" Mrs. Foster asked.

"Derrick's graduating from medical school this year, he's probably getting some tips," I replied.
Mrs. Foster just continued to stare and said, "Oh."
The Three Musketeers came back in the house and continued to chat about medical ailments. Mr. Foster pointed to Derrick and said, "Honey, Derrick is going to be a..."

Mrs. Foster cut him off, "A doctor, yes, Shanelle told me." She looked at Derrick and said, "Congrats to you Derrick." He looked slightly embarrassed and quietly thanked her.

I knelt down and grabbed Troy by the shoulders.

"Be good for Nana and Pop Pop, I'll pick you up tomorrow."

"Okay mommy, I love you."

"I love you too baby, don't forget to call me to say night night."

"Okay, mommy, Troy don't forget."

Mr. Foster walked us to the car and said, "Listen, I'm grilling tomorrow after church, so stay a while. Tammy's in town and she's going back tomorrow. She's been asking for you Shanelle."

"Well, I won't make any promises, but we'll try."

Cocoa Brown Skin

Derrick and I returned to a quiet house. When we got inside, it took him a while to get comfortable, so I immediately showed him the guest room and bathroom to unwind from the beach. It was already four o'clock so I started taking out vegetables and marinated meat. I wasn't sure what Derrick wanted to do with our time, so I turned on Kiss FM to break up some of the tension. I think we both knew we were going to hit the sheets, but I wasn't sure how or when. He came downstairs looking absolutely delicious. A fresh shower enhanced his cocoa brown skin and smooth exterior. Harold Melvin and the Blue Notes were playing on the radio. Derrick started laughing and said, "You used to be my girl, now you're my lady."

I started laughing and said, "I like the sound of that." There was confidence in my voice as I looked around the kitchen. Having him there with me enticed my energy and longing for him. Derrick walked up from behind me and said, "I like the sound of that too."

I put my cooking utensils down and turned around to face him. I looked in his eyes and said, "This feels like déjà vu."

Derrick stroked my neck and slowly rested his forehead against mine. In a deep voice he said, "It does

Shanelle, but I just don't know how to make it right. I don't even know if you really want me, this is your world not mine."

I grabbed his face as we began to breath in unison.

"I want you to feel comfortable Derrick, you're more than welcome here."

My sentence seemed pretty convincing as Derrick picked me up and sat me on the counter top. I grabbed his face again and whispered to him, hoping that it would settle his nerves.

"We can go somewhere else if you like, but I want you here with me."

Derrick looked me in the eyes and then began to brush his baby stubble against my face. He placed his hands on my waist and began to slide them up until his thumbs rested on my nipples. My response was immediate as I pulled into him and stroked his back. We began to breathe heavier and heavier as Derrick slid his hands back down and rested them at my waist. The softest kiss followed his embrace as my eyes began to close. He slid his tongue into my mouth which created an immediate blood rush to Kitty. I wanted him to squeeze my breasts but he avoided them, making sure to rub my nipples ever so slightly with his thumbs. The sensation made me crave him in greater intensity as I made love to his tongue. Suddenly, the phone rang, but we continued to kiss. Derrick massaged my back and called my name as I continued to ignore the phone.

"Are you going to get that?" He whispered.

I didn't want to, but I did with a quick and steady voice.

"Hello."

"Hi mommy!"

Derrick backed away as my arms reached out for him. I jumped down from off the counter to temporarily talk to my son, who suddenly seemed annoying to me. I leaned on the counter and tried to multitask two issues; Derrick's wonderful touch and whatever my wonderful two year old wanted.

"Yes sweetie, you having fun?" Derrick laughed and teased my English as he whispered back, "Are you having fun?"

"Troy having fun mommy, I love you."

I playfully smacked Derrick and said, "I love you too, call mommy when it's time for night night?"

"Okay, mommy." Troy said.

Derrick stood in front of me and held me as Mr. Foster began to speak.

"Sorry to bother you Shanelle, he missed you."

A slight paused followed.

"Shanelle, are you there?"

"Yeah, I'm here, thanks for calling dad, I told Troy to call me when he's ready for bed, goodbye."

I hung the phone up and looked at Derrick. He silenced me by taking the phone out of my hands and placed it back on the cradle. In a warm and intimate gesture, Derrick grabbed my hand and pressed his fingers into my palm. He held it up and kissed it, carefully embracing each finger with a gentle massage. My heart started to race as I watched him entice every organ in my body to stand up and pay attention. He held my hand against his heart and started to kiss me again. After a while he had no choice but to put me back on the countertop because he was taller than I was. Derrick paused for a moment and stared at me. We shared a smile and then a quick laugh as our foreheads rested against each other. He was breathing heavy, but he was in control. He looked into my eyes and said, "I wonder how much time will pass before we can start saying I love you."

"I don't know Derrick," I replied, "But I trust you

and I'm willing to take a chance." I held my lips next to his and said, "Will you take a chance with me?"

Derrick cupped my face with his hands and softly whispered, "Yes."

Our eyes closed in relief as he pressed his lips against mine and whispered, "We're older now and the stakes are higher this time, are you sure Shanelle?"

Suddenly, the subject shifted. I knew he was referring to us being intimate. I sealed his answer with a kiss and said, "Yes, I'm sure, Derrick, it's time, even though you know I need my space."

He looked at me and slowly moved his head up and down. "All the space in the world, no pressure."

He released my hand and flipped it over to look at my palm again. Derrick took his pointer finger and began to trace the lines. I caressed his face with my free hand and stared at his warm demeanor. Derrick kissed me on the neck and inhaled. The intensity in his touch was so overwhelming that I pulled him into me and began to squeeze him. His neck and chest emitted so much heat that my nipples immediately became erect again through my shirt. The feel of his skin against me led me straight to the floor and into his arms again for another warm embrace.

Without saying a word, we walked upstairs to the guestroom. The master bedroom was off limits to the outside world. There were too many memories for me to feel guilty about if I slept with Derrick. In my heart, I felt like the time was right, but not in a room that was filled with love. I think if the door was open, I would have abandoned the idea. Holding Derrick's hand and trusting him the way I did was the support I needed for the moment.

We went into the guest bedroom and quietly looked around. Responsibilities came next as Derrick headed for his bag and pulled out some condoms. He smiled and said, "We won't call it safe sex, how about safe lovin'?"

"Pure genius," I said, as I stood at the edge of the bed. Derrick sat down and grabbed my hands.

"Are you ok?" He asked.

"I'm fine," I replied as I stroked his cheeks. "I'm going to take a shower."

Derrick had other plans as he stared at me. "Don't hide in the bathroom, take your clothes off right here."

The insecurities I used to feel were long gone as I began to pull my shirt over my head. I waited for him to respond and he did with a steady smile as he used his pointer finger to slide my bra strap off my shoulders. Derrick continued to seduce me with his eyes as he placed his hands behind my back and unhooked my bra. He watched it fall to the floor and slowly raised his eyes to meet mine.

Derrick quietly whispered to me, "Come closer Shanelle, you're too far."

He was too seductive to resist as I stepped in between his legs. Derrick wrapped one arm around my waist and pulled me into him with a soft bite into my left breast. He grabbed my hand as I looked up into the ceiling and moaned out loud. Derrick skillfully slid my thong down with his right hand as it quickly fell to the floor. His hand settled into Kitty's den and he explored me from behind with his determined hands. He was pleased to find so much nectar within his reach and spread it onto my inner thighs. Derrick turned me around and bit my back with soft intensity. After that, he pulled me onto his lap and explored the rest of me with his hands. The feeling was so overwhelming I wanted to turn around and kiss him, but I also wanted to enjoy his exploration. The need to take a shower diminished as I turned around and straddled his lap. We looked into each other's eyes and smiled. No voices permeated my thoughts or riddled my conscience. They say timing is everything and it certainly held true for us. Before he took me, Derrick wrapped his arms around me in a warm embrace. Tears welled up in my eyes as our skin pressed together. Derrick serenaded me with a whisper to let me know how he felt.

"Shanelle, you feel so incredible, I want this feeling to last forever."

Goosebumps swirled up my back as I squeezed him tight and responded to his feelings.

"I want you Derrick, take me. Take me now."

Without hesitation, Derrick laid me down and put all of his weight on me. He spread my legs with his hand and slid it along my thighs as he moaned in pleasure. I slowly wrapped my hands around his neck and took a deep breath.

Derrick smelled wonderful and his cocoa brown skin felt tight and smooth. The feel of him against my skin was just the right touch as I bit my lower lip and stared at him. I let go of him so he could remove his shorts and adorn himself with protection. Sure, it wasn't the real thing, but it was a safe, healthy start.

Derrick grabbed my hand and entered me slow and steady as I responded to the feel of his manhood. He quickly enticed my nipples to respond to him by rubbing each one in small circles as he rhythmically rocked me to and fro. Derrick was well endowed. I found myself repositioning my hips to keep up with the initial pain I felt for him. He laid down on top of me and bit my earlobe as he called my name. Derrick stared deep into my eyes and gently kissed my lips. Hard thrusts complimented the feel of his tongue. The feeling was so pleasurable, my thighs tightened and supported his movements. I stroked his lower back and whispered his name a million times as he answered by squeezing my hand. Derrick turned me over and spread me apart across the bed. He kissed me in places that stirred up new arousals as my fingers gripped the sheets upon entry. He slid his hand under my stomach to support his entry as I moaned for him. In a deep and steady voice, Derrick whispered in my ear and increased my pleasure with his words.

"I can't believe I'm inside of you Shanelle. I don't want this to end."

The way he made love to me seemed endless as Derrick mixed words and exploration together. In just the right places, Derrick caressed and touched me like I was a work of art. His love of the human body took me to heights of physical pleasure. Derrick massaged my pressure points and pleasure points at the same time. He placed his hand under my lower back and talked me through my first orgasm. We locked hands while he told me to breath through my nose and focus on my pleasure. He encouraged me to be free with him by stroking my nipples. When I did, Derrick became more aroused which extended our time as one being. He stared me straight in the eyes and responded to all of my facial expressions. We used our own energy to create a symphony of dim lights and soft music. Derrick began to triple in size as he told me to hold him before he released himself inside of me. Goose bumps riddled his upper arms as I dug my nails into his skin. Laying next to him covered in sweat was all I needed as he pulled me into his arms. I laid on his chest and smoothed his silky hair as he stroked my butt with the tips of his fingers.

"Shanelle," he whispered, "What did you do to me?"

As I tried to catch my breath I replied, "What did you do to me?"

He paused briefly and said, "I'm so glad we waited."

MMOODY HOLIDAY** **MOODY HOLIDAY** **MOODY HOLIDAY** 139

"Why?" I asked.

"Even after all this time, you are so pure and passionate. I like the way you respond to me and yourself." He cleared his throat and sat up while I repositioned my body on top of his. Derrick smiled as he looked at me.

"You're just you, there's nothing fake or pretentious about you and I love that."

A gentle smile from me complimented his feelings as he squeezed me tight. Derrick continued, "It's not just making love either Shanelle. You and I missed out on a lot of fun. We had to grow up fast. I'm not trying to get that back, but it feels good being with someone who understands my serious and silly ways."

I sighed and said, "Just don't forget Troy, there's no me without him."

Before Derrick could respond, the phone rang. I picked up the phone and said, "Hello."

"Hi mommy!"

"Hi Troy," I replied with a wide grin on my face.

"Are you going night night now?"

Derrick stroked my face as I waited for an answer.

"Yes, mommy."

Derrick said, "Tell him I said goodnight."

I handed him the phone and he obliged.

"Hey man, are you going to bed?"

"Hi Mr. Dee, I go to bed now."

"Goodnight," Derrick said.

"Night, night," Troy said.

Derrick reached over and hung up the phone as I snuggled in tighter to his lean frame.

Derrick stretched his body out and said, "I'm starving, are you hungry?"

"No, I'm happy."

He playfully smacked me on the butt and said, "Is

that the secret? If it is, I hope you stay that way because you look and feel great to me." Derrick yawned and said, "Well, I'm going to make myself at home and fix something to eat. I also need to hit the books if you don't mind."

"That's fine, book worm." I replied. I watched him get up and head for the shower as I pulled the covers up to my chin. Parts of me tingled all over thinking about the love we made. In retrospect, maturity and time did us some good. Derrick was right, the time we spent that night was more fulfilling to me than any feelings I had for him so long ago. Thinking of him forced me to my feet and into the shower. The minute he saw my naked frame he started laughing.

"Here she comes, trouble!"

"What?" I said, as I stepped inside with a silly grin on my face.

"Admit it Shanelle, you can't resist me in a shower. Matter of fact, I think it was the last time I saw you naked, until tonight."

I started laughing as Derrick wrapped his arms around me and squeezed me tight.

"Yeah, I was a girl on the run, but you took good care of me." I looked into his eyes and melted at the thought of how much he respected me back then. "You also honored my wishes and that was sweet of you Derrick."

Derrick grabbed my face and said, "Shanelle, with the things you were going through, that was the right thing to do. I'm just glad that we're together again."

Water pellets struck my face as Derrick brushed them away with his thumb. We hugged each other again and stayed in a tight embrace. He felt wonderful in my arms and I didn't want to let him go. Down below, Mr. Mighty bellowed up again as Derrick pulled my body into his manhood.

I started laughing and said, "What kind of vitamins are you taking?"

Derrick knelt down and bit me on my butt. He looked up at me as streams of water splashed on his face. "Ah," he replied. "Roots and herbs in my tea gal." He laughed out loud and said, "Don't leave me hanging Shanelle."

I wrapped my arms around him and rocked him back and forth. "This isn't a big shower Derrick."

He didn't answer, instead he stepped outside and wrapped me up in a towel. We went back into the bedroom for a second round of lovemaking.

Stamina got the best of me as I enjoyed his playful tongue against Kitty. My orgasm forced his erection inside of me with screaming pleasure as he put my legs on his shoulders. He never took his eyes off of me as he rocked me into the late evening. By the time we finished, Derrick was rejuvenated for three hours of studying into the early morning as I slept with a smooth smile on my face.

I woke up to the smell of a cheese omelet. I took a long hot bath before I joined Derrick downstairs. Fatigue was in his eyes but he looked peaceful.

"Get any studying in?" I asked, as I kissed him on the forehead.

He pinched me on the arm and said, "I had no choice, now I need some sleep."

I was so spanked by Derrick's lovemaking, I didn't care what he did. "Okay, I didn't make any plans today, so relax. Besides, you need to rest before the ride back."

"Are you going to the cookout?" Derrick asked.

"For a little while. You don't have to go if you want to."

"Good," Derrick replied, "I need some sleep."

"Well," I said, "I'm going to get this place cleaned

up and pack for the week. I have a few chapters to read and then I'll go over to the cookout."

Derrick shook his head and said, "That'll work, are you staying at Candy's tonight?"

"Yes," I replied.

"Well, we'll leave together then."

Having my own down time without Troy felt great. I cleaned up in no time and quickly packed his bag for the week. Without thought, I walked into the master bedroom and suddenly paused. There was brevity in the room as thoughts of Alex appeared in the photographs we shared with each other. I picked up his photo and stared at him. There was comfort in my heart for him as I dusted the glass containing his picture. I placed it next to Troy's baby picture and continued to clean up the room until the phone rang.

"Oh, hey Shanelle, it's me Tammy, I was getting ready to hang up."

"No, I'm here, what's up? Better yet, what's Troy doing?"

My question seemed to calm her agitation. "He just came back from church with mom and dad. What are you doing?" she asked.

"Cleaning up," I replied, as I peeked in on Derrick.

"Well," Tammy said, "I wanted to come by and talk before the cookout."

I stepped back from the guestroom. "No," I said, "We can talk later."

"Shanelle," Tammy said, "I hope you're not holding a grudge."

I shook my head and said, "No Tammy, I have company."

A twenty-second pause followed. I think I was blowing the Fosters away with all of my revelations, but I felt like the truth was a better resolve than avoidance.

"Oh, well I'll talk to you when you get here."

"No problem, I said, "Can you tell ma to put Troy down for a nap at two o'clock, I won't be staying long when I come."

Tammy didn't question my motives. "Okay Shanelle."

I hung up the phone and peeked in on Derrick again. He was sound asleep and stretched out across the bed. There was confidence in my gait as I headed down the stairs to finish a few more chores. I thought to myself, "Things are getting better as each day goes by."

Shanelle versus Tammy

Troy was the first person to greet me at the door when I arrived at the Fosters. There was relief in Mrs. Foster's eyes when she saw me coming through the door solo. She wasn't ready for Derrick and her greeting to me was a reminder.

"Girl, this child is just like his father. He wants and wants until he gets it." She threw her head back but cut her smile off as she headed for the kitchen. Tammy came downstairs next as Troy sat on my lap for me to tie his shoes. She was a sight to see. She must have gained forty pounds and her face was riddled with acne. To boot, her eyes were blood shot red. She sat down next to me and smiled as she helped me tie Troy's other shoe.

"So," she said, "You're headed back to North Orange?"

"Why?" I asked. I was in defensive mode as I put Troy on the floor.

"I dropped out and they don't want me here."

"Why did you drop out?" I asked.

"Long story," Tammy replied.

Troy started walking to the kitchen. The smell of Mrs. Foster's biscuits always forced him to his feet. I turned to Tammy and said, "Nikki?"

"Alex is gone, but you're starting to sound like him," Tammy said.

"So what does all of this have to do with me?" I asked.

"I need a place to stay," Tammy said.

"Well you can stay at the house…"

Tammy cut me off, "No, I mean up there."

"North Orange?" My question was filled with surprise.

Tammy looked excited when she answered. In fact, she looked as desperate as I did back in the day. I remained poised and said, "Where's Nikki, in North Orange?"

Tammy stood up and said, "I'm not sweatin' her, please Shanelle, get serious."

I stood up to her and said, "Well where is she now?"

Tammy put her head down and said, "North Orange."

My head calculated Tammy's demise. "She's got you all strung out, weeded up, sexed up, don't know if you're coming or going on any given day."

Tammy sucked her teeth and rolled her eyes. She didn't respond because she wanted me to say yes and I wasn't giving in so easily.

"Huh?" Tammy replied.

I put my arm on her shoulder and said, "Look Tammy, I'm staying with Candy until I get a place and it's going to be awhile. Why don't you get a job down here and get your head together…"

"No! Stop trying to tell me what to do Shanelle. Look at you, you got your life all figured out now, new man chillin' at your house, cute kid, money, nice car…"

"Tammy please, you don't know me, you may

think you do, but you don't. Besides, you need to worry about yourself and figure out what you want instead of chasing Nikki."

Tammy rolled her eyes again and walked upstairs. I went to the backyard and ate a small salad. Trust me, the entire family were watching, but food wasn't an issue anymore. As long as there was no stress around, I was okay. This time Tammy was peering from her window looking down at me wishing she was free.

"I can't stay Ma," I said, "I've got to get back on the road."

Troy took my cue and slid off the bench while he waved goodbye. Mrs. Foster looked pissed off, but there was nothing I could do to please her either. She grabbed Troy by the wrist and squeezed him tight. He patted her back and said, "Next time Nana, Troy be back."

Mrs. Foster looked up at me as she struggled away from her grandson's embrace. Her next sentence confirmed her suspicion. "Why don't you make a plate for Derrick too."

I smiled at her confidently and said, "Thanks, maybe I will."

Mr. Foster was the only one who understood me. He gave me a plastic bag and walked me to my car.

"I'm glad you're going to keep the house Shanelle, you'll be glad you did. Call me with the address to your mother's house. I'll be down tomorrow and take a look at it before I put in a bid."

Hearing him say "your mother," froze me into temporary shock. I looked at him and said, "It's a long story, but in my life, she's only Vivian to me."

With all the secrets he had during the course of his life, Mr. Foster didn't ask any questions.

Troy climbed into his carseat as I wrapped my arms tightly around Mr. Foster's neck. "We'll be home

Saturday morning okay dad?"

He blinked his eyes to force back tears for his whole family and said, "Okay, Shanelle, see you Saturday." Mr. Foster stuck his hand through the window and tickled Troy's stomach while Troy fought him off with a high pitched laugh. He stood on the sidewalk and watched us pull off with a smile on his face. I was glad he understood. In time, the rest of them would heal too.

Time Heals

Life pulled a fast forward on all of us in a matter of months. A quiet sale with a Ten Thousand dollar profit sent Mrs. Viv packing to Virginia. Needless to say, she took Steven with her. With what little money she had, Steven was transferred to a long term care facility just outside of Fredericksburg. Little remorse rested in my heart for him and Mrs. Viv. I quietly disconnected them and went along with my life like I was supposed to do. Alex would have wanted that for us. Besides, the Fosters were like surrogate parents to me even when the chips were down.

Speaking of parents, when Candy couldn't button her jeans anymore, she finally announced that she was pregnant. We didn't have the nerve to tell her we knew just by the sight of her nose. It spread across her face so fast, we were convinced she was having a girl. As a result, Derrick and Clinton had ample opportunities to exchange small talk about raising children. Candy was more than happy to stay home during her pregnancy because the sight of food and cooking oil made her sick all the time. She didn't have the courage to board an airplane and tend to needy people on tight airline flights.

Mr. Foster hired the best licensed contractors in town and gutted the house from top to bottom. By the time the house was complete, there were no haunting memories at the front door or in the attic. Butter cream paint with white trim coated the living room and dining room walls. Crown molding blazed a beautiful ascent up the staircase that use to be worn away from Steven's early obsession. Solid wooden doors graced the bedrooms that use to lock at night from Steven's perpetual thievery. The attic, by design was converted into a bright day room with bursting beams of sun from an oval skylight. The third floor became a colorful sanctuary graced with colorful paintings I purchased from a famous Bahamian artist.

Against my better judgment, on the first day of spring, I let Tammy move in on the third floor while I continued my classes at St. James. Her college dreams at Pitt were long gone and she was looking for direction from anyone who understood her immediate cause.

Tammy's weight doubled during our grieving for Alex. Nikki crept in and out her life behind our backs and the Fosters accepted my departure as long as I kept an eye out for Tammy. I made a pact with Tammy to help her get on her feet while she lived with me for six months. Even though I didn't need the money, I made her pay rent to keep her disciplined. She got a job at a dental office on South Center Street and registered for classes at St. James. A ten minute walk in either direction was just the right kind of exercise for her weight gain.

Tammy was three semesters short of a degree and looked to me for determination to finish. We kept our class schedules on the refrigerator to keep up with one another and every now and then I let her babysit her nephew. I had to remind her about leaving junk food in the house. It was disturbing to watch her put on weight so fast. I tried to get her to focus, but smoking weed got in her way. She learned her way around North Orange real quick and picked up weed in the Valley before she came home. I never saw or smelled it in the house, but Derrick and I could see it in her slanted red eyes. Whenever Derrick came around, she turned into Medusa as evil snakes hissed and cajoled at his mere presence. Derrick liked Tammy, but he was suspicious of my codependency.

"Shanelle," he said one night over flirty phone banter, "Every time I come over there she's high. Now don't tell me you don't notice?"

"I do notice."

"Well, are you going to do something about it?" Derrick asked.

"Derrick, I gave her six months to get her act together and that's it. She's got to get her own place, she knows that already."

"Shanelle," Derrick said. "I'm not telling you what to do, but you've got Troy to worry about first." I didn't want to worry Derrick with my simple life. He was studying around the clock and getting ready for graduation. I didn't think it was fair for him to take on my responsibilities.

I smiled at his answer. "Well look at you getting all protective over my son."

"Please Shanelle, you know that's my little man and I'm going to look out for him and his stubborn mama."

"Oh now I'm a mama?' I asked.

"Yeah," he said, "My sexy mama."

I blew Derrick a kiss over the phone. There wasn't much else that needed to be said because we both needed to hit the books. He mentioned one more thing before he hung up the phone.

"I have to start looking for apartments in Jersey Shanelle. My lease is up in two months."

"When does your residency start?" I asked.

"Late July," Derrick replied.

"What about your mother?"

"Shanelle, don't even go there."

"Okay, you'll figure it out Derrick. Get through your finals and graduation, something will come up," I said.

The next day I headed for class. A notice caught my eyes from the political science bulletin board.

"Internships available in Washington, only two slots left. See Professor Jeffries."

Without hesitation, I snatched the notice off the board and headed to his office.

"Hi Professor Jeffries."

He peered above his glasses and said, "Shanelle, what brings you here?"

I handed him the notice and said, "I would like to go to Washington, what do I need to do?"

He smiled and said, "Great, can you get me a writing sample and resume tomorrow morning?"

"I'll get it for you today."

He held up his hands and said, "I'm sure you'll have no problem, what's your GPA?"

I held my head up and said, "A three point forty-five sir."

"That's even better." Professor Jeffries scribbled my name on a post it note and stuck it to his computer.

"Bring it tomorrow and I'll give you the slip to register."

I felt lightheaded and happy as I walked out of the building. A pay phone in the distance led me straight to Derrick.

"Washington? That was quick, I just hung up with you yesterday." Derrick said.

I held the particulars in my hand and said, "The

Children's Advocacy Center, 1500 M Street Washington, D.C."

Derrick laughed and said, "Can you take Troy to work too?"

My heart immediately dropped to floor. I forgot a big piece of the puzzle.

"Shanelle?" Derrick asked. "Are you there?"

"Oh, yeah I'm here. Damn, I forgot I had a son!"

Derrick's sarcasm got the best of him as he took his turn at questioning me, "So what are you going to do Miss Shanelle?"

My mind quickly raced with strategy. *"Let's see, I can't rely on Tammy, I need her to watch the house, Candy's getting too tired and cranky to take her with me. Derrick has no apartment and doesn't start until late July..."*

"Come with me!" I shouted.

"Me?" Derrick asked.

"Yeah, well you're going to be homeless in two months and you need to take a break after you take your exams. Besides your residency doesn't start until July." I jumped up and down as I grabbed the cord, "C'mon, help a sista out!"

Derrick started laughing and said, "We can't afford to go Shanelle."

Derrick didn't know what I was worth, so I kept him at bay just to see if he would be down for the struggle.

"I get by with Alex's Social Security checks, we can swing it."

Derrick hesitated at first and said, "Well, I know a few people in Silver Springs, Maryland. Let me make a few phone calls."

"So you're going with us?" I asked.

"Is that what you want?" Derrick questioned.

"Of course!" I shouted.

"Well, you only live once, let's go," Derrick replied.

I placed my hand on the phone and said, "Derrick."

"Yeah," he replied.

"Thank you," I said.

Shanelle Goes to Washington

"Washington!" Mrs. Foster shouted, "Shanelle, can you just focus on one thing at a time?"

Mr. Foster wedged himself between us with his hands on his hips.

"No!" I yelled back. "I can focus on as many things as I want. I'm twenty-three now and the last time I checked, I don't have to answer to anyone."

Mrs. Foster's facial expression was unforgiving.

"Well what about Troy, do you mean to tell me he's going with you?" she asked.

"Of course he is, he's my son and I'm not leaving him behind."

She was quickly losing control as she rubbed at an ulcer fermenting in her stomach. I couldn't read her mind and I knew I couldn't please her by saying, "Okay, I'll stay." I cleared the strain and worry from my face and stood strong.

"You need to understand that I'm trying to move on with my life. Maybe I looked settled when Alex was here, but I gave up so many things that I don't want to regret ever again. Derrick and I are going to work out Troy's needs and he'll be fine. But if I decide to do a

million things all at once, I'm entitled." I caught my
breath and pleaded with their emotions. "I said before you
guys are the only family Troy has. What I meant to say is
that you're all the family we have, so please don't turn
your back on me now."

Mrs. Foster held her hands to her mouth and began
to cry. Mr. Foster pulled us into a huddle and she
immediately grabbed me. I whispered in her ear to
reassure her self-doubt.

"I promise, we're coming back Mom."

When she released me, Mr. Foster handed her a
wilted tissue from his pocket. She laughed at the sight of
it, but immediately wiped her tears away as she sighed.
Mr. Foster looked at me and said, "We couldn't ask for a
spunkier daughter-in-law Shanelle. We'll be fine, it's just
taking this ole' girl more time to adjust that's all. You have
our blessings."

That evening, Troy stayed overnight with his
grandparents while I packed. I kissed Alex's picture and
quietly talked to him while I straightened up my bedroom.
The doorbell rang and I knew it was Derrick. I bolted
down the stairs and opened up the door with a beaming
smile on my face. When he saw me he leaned back and
said, "Somebody's really happy to see me!" I pulled him
inside the house and squeezed the life out of him.

"Hmm, you feel so good holding me Derrick."

He rubbed my back and said, "Okay, okay, I'll hold
you."

I looked up at him and said, "For once everything
is going my way and the right way."

He kissed my forehead with his warm lips and
said, "It's a good feeling when you put your mind to
something you believe in."

I stood on my tippy toes, kissed his lips and

replied, "You're right."

Derrick smacked me on my butt and said, "Alright woman, let's rustle up some food, I'm starving."

Derrick and I sampled so much food during the preparation, we were full by the time it was finished. He didn't care and neither did I as we shared a glass of wine on the kitchen floor. We knew we had a long trip ahead of us with Troy in tow but we didn't care. A thundershower began to fall and we quickly ran around the house to shut all the open windows. By the time we caught up with each other, we were at the top of the staircase breathing heavily. Derrick looked me in the eyes and grabbed me by the waist. I lifted his shirt up with a feeling of new found independence. Once his shirt hit the floor, I told him to lie down. He found humor in my request and got down on his knees instead. He lifted my shirt and began to kiss my belly button as I stroked his hair.

"Before I lay down, you promise you won't hurt me?" Derrick asked.

My head tilted back in uproarious laughter. I grabbed his chin and said, "I'll be gentle baby, lay down."

I quickly ran to the bedroom and found a condom sitting in my lingerie drawer. When I came back, Derrick placed his hands behind his head and let me take over. I put my hand over his mouth when I mounted him and watched his face relax with unbridled pleasure. Derrick palmed my butt and rocked me to and fro as we started to sweat uncontrollably. Fearing a rugburn to my knees, we ran to the bedroom and finished our lovemaking on cool white sheets. Derrick's brawn took over as he laid me down and wrapped my legs around his neck. I grabbed the bedrails and stretched my body out to feel his full intensity and thrust. It seemed like it was never going to end, but when it did, I let out a scream of pure enjoyment as my body broke down into a shivering heap of happiness.

Derrick kissed my toes, earlobes, hips and inner thighs as I begged him to hold me. When he did, he wiped the sweat off my forehead and said, "Shanelle, you're a piece of work." He got up and opened the window to let a cool breeze quiet our frenzy. While I nestled into a deep sleep, Derrick took a shower and packed the jeep. By the time he climbed into bed, I was balled up tight. Derrick rubbed my body up and down until I melted into his frame for a good night sleep.

The beauty of being young and carefree never felt real to me until our trip to Washington. We packed the Jeep with last minute items, including Troy, who was singing in the backseat for the drive down. A couple of good connections made our transition easy too. Clinton knew a pilot who was looking for someone to sublease his apartment in Georgetown for three months while he vacationed in Europe. Since we were considered good friends of Clinton, we were lucky enough to get by without a security deposit. I gave the check to Candy to cover three months rent and told Derrick that Mr. Foster was handling my expenses. Derrick still needed to feel like the man of the house so he picked up a research assignment at D.C. General.

By day I was researching child care legislation and preparing a database for the agency. It was arduous work, but I loved every minute of my time in the office. Every night, Derrick and Troy met me at the Metro station so Troy could enjoy his time on the train. He loved it so much, he cried everytime we got off.

Derrick was patient with Troy. He was stern with him, but at the same time nurturing and consistent. Deep inside of Derrick's heart, I knew he was reliving the childhood he never had with his father. From the looks of things, Troy was a lucky little boy.

We went out to dinner at least two nights a week

once Derrick started receiving a paycheck. Being in the heart of Georgetown forced Derrick and I into great political debates and wonderful lovemaking at night. We fell in love in D.C. and we knew it without saying it.

Back at home, paint fumes, or the voice of Steven began to possess Tammy's soul on the third floor. During the fifth week of my internship, she called Nikki for a Friday night pleasure party.

"Fuck it," Tammy said, "Bring whatever and whoever, let's do this."

Private parties in a college town spread quickly, even during summer session. Since Nikki went both ways, she made a few phone calls on both sides of the track. By eight o'clock, a medium sized eclectic crowd began to trickle into my newly decorated home with weed, Hennesy and Colt 45 in tow. Of course, Nikki called Flaco to bring in the good shit and he was more than delighted to crash my pad and smell my sheets for a turn on.

"Where's Shanelle?" Flaco asked.

"Just come on dummy, I wouldn't be asking you if she was here. She's in D.C."

"Aight, aight," Flaco replied. "I'll be right over." When he got to my house, Flaco and Nikki went upstairs to roll a blunt. Nikki excused herself on the second floor to use the bathroom and told Flaco to wait. His innate scent of a woman lead him to my room with sinister eyes. He surveyed my bed and opened my dresser drawers. A pair of pink panties went into his jean pocket before he walked out to meet Nikki. He laughed to himself thinking, *"Weed and pussy, two of my favorite things."*

Before Nikki opened the door to the bathroom, a pair of keys caught his attention. He quickly shoved them into his pocket. My panties muffled the jingle as Nikki opened the door and looked into his mischievous eyes. All Flaco could think about was the day he could let himself back into my house and finish what he started so long ago.

Nikki and Flaco headed to the third floor while Tammy worked her way through the crowd downstairs. She went into the kitchen and found a pretty brown skinned sister searching for a snack.

"Looking for something to eat?" Tammy asked. She closed the refrigerator door and eyed Tammy's boyish charm up and down with a seductive smile.

"I was hoping someone could eat me," she said.

Tammy was taken aback at first, but then she batted her eyes and thought about Nikki's whereabouts. Tammy smiled as she envisioned herself with the brown buttercup. Tammy extended her hand and led her upstairs. She called Nikki down from the attic and whispered their intentions. Nikki looked the temptress up and down and said, "Don't I know you?"

She grabbed Nikki and Tammy's hand and said, "Does it matter?"

Nikki shook her head and replied with glazed over eyes, "No, not at all."

The three of them went into the bathroom and fired up a blunt while Nikki watched Tammy and the familiar girl freak each other out in my brand new bathroom equipped with a new shower head. Tammy took the shower head off the cradle and rocked herself off with fast pellets while the temptress bit at various body parts below her waist.

Meanwhile, Flaco was laying on his back on Tammy's bed in the attic. He had the best high of all as he stared at the ceiling. A defect in the contractor's job after the installation of the skylight caused excess rainwater to puddle into a soft spot in the ceiling. In a matter of weeks, the moisture dried up and formed a brown shape that looked like a T-Rex dinosaur in Flaco's hazed vision. Flaco's paranoia found it funny at first, but the more he stared, the dinosaur began to grow razor sharp teeth. He blinked twice and tried to focus on the laughter from downstairs. Once his eyes were in focus, he noticed that the image was still there. Flaco slowly turned his head to the nightstand and picked up a small stress ball. He threw the ball at the spot and covered his eyes when debris began to fall on his face. The ball smacked him in his mouth and forced some of the material onto his tastebuds. He quickly reacted by sitting up and wiping his tongue off with Tammy's quilt. He threw the ball up again out of curiosity. This time, the physical force of his throw lodged it into the ceiling. Flaco rubbed his nose and stood up to study the wreckage. The intensity of his high caused him to start peeling and pulling away at the sheet rock until a six inch piece gave way revealing a tin box. Flaco jumped up on the bed and tapped the box with his fingers until it fell and bounced on the bed. He immediately got up and closed the door for privacy. When he opened the box, to his surprise, the three missing glocks and empty crack viles Steven stole out of Mama Barb's apartment were inside and ready for the taking. Flaco held one gun in each hand and simply replied, "Word up."

His next move infuriated Rico.

"What the fuck do you mean you're at Shanelle's house? Mother fucker, take the guns, hang up the damn phone and get the fuck out of there!"

The damage had already been done. As high as Flaco was, he thought he was doing a noble thing calling Rico. But as he hung up the phone, his dazed state of affairs caused him to drop the gun on the floor. The fully loaded glock dislodge and fired a shot into the ceiling.

Startled by the noise and his own stupidity, Flaco ran downstairs, leaving the third gun, including his fingerprints.

Back in the bathroom, the pretty stranger quickly

jumped out of the shower and said, "What was that noise?" Nikki passed her a towel and said, "That's my cousin goofing around."

Tammy quickly reacted, "Flaco's here?"

Nikki sucked her teeth and said, "Well you said whoever, whatever."

Sensing the tension, the temptress quickly put her clothes on to leave. Tammy grabbed her arm and said, "Wait, don't go."

She laughed and said, "It was cute, but that sounded like a gun shot, I have to go."

Nikki smiled and grabbed her by the waist. She traced her finger along her panty line and then zipped up her jeans. Nikki smiled and said, "You never told me your name."

She opened the door, flipped her long hair back and said, "Portia."

The commotion from the third floor, including Flaco's quick haul ass exit from my house sent everyone running for the exit. Neighbors immediately called the police.

"Yes that's what I said, I heard a gunshot at the Brown's house, 122 Crescent Avenue." The anonymous neighbor sighed in frustration and said, "Oh, it's been a while, but they're at it again."

Countdown to Flaco

Two pictures hung on the evidence wall at Newark Police Department's homicide division. One was a mug shot of Flaco and the other photo was Rico's. Alex's murder investigation was left up to the local police, but a liaison from the feds was assigned just in case there were any left over issues from the sting operation.

Andre's tip was critical. Even though they had the case wrapped up in eight months, they needed to nail Rico as a co-conspirator. By the time a wire tap was granted, Rico said very little about the killing. As far as Rico was concerned, the job was done and there was nothing left to talk about. Although silence protected him for the moment, Flaco's flagrant stupidity opened up a new can of worms.

"So what do we have so far?" the chief of homicide asked. "I need to put this case on the table tomorrow and issue a warrant for Flaco Santiago's arrest."

A slim veteran detective placed a file on the table and said, "It's a solid case, we've got his fingerprints in both cars and the wood shrapnel found next to the corpse in Building One on Freeway Drive matches the shrapnel found in the shooter's duffel bag. The drive to Shiloh was

162

three miles chief, we have video surveillance tape of both suspects leaving McDonald's on Broad Street twenty minutes before the wedding started. Tire treads from the..."

The heavy set chief stood up and adjusted his belt. "Look, we need more, I don't need the word "circumstantial" following this case, we have a dead officer to answer for, you got that?"

The liaison assigned to Alex's murder investigation stood up to receive a phone call.

"Shots fired, how many? Who's responding? Okay, I'm on my way."

A room full of homicide detectives stood up to hear the agent's lead. As he shoved his arm through his sleeves he stated, "We've got shots fired at 122 Crescent Avenue. They want the task force assigned. As soon as I have more information, I'll let you know."

Tammy was too afraid to call me in D.C. while the police and the feds scoured the third floor for fingerprints and ballistics information. A call came in an hour later with the information. Three sets of fingerprints matched Flaco's; one on the door, the abandoned gun and ceiling. The liaison quickly ran downstairs and began to interrogate Tammy.

"Look, we all know who you are, so tell me something, why would you let him into your sister-in-law's house for a party?"

Snot drizzled down Tammy's red nose. "I didn't know he was here, Nikki invited him!"

"Nikki huh?" the officer sarcastically stated.

Tammy wiped her nose and said, "Yeah, why?"

"C'mon now, your family kept a low profile for the entire trial, you don't think you're putting Shanelle and yourself in jeopardy by hanging out with them?"

Tammy didn't answer. The officer immediately

pulled a card out his pocket and said, "Kid, pack up and go home, Lakewood right?"

"Yes," Tammy quivered.

"We need to talk to Shanelle again, and I don't think she's going to be too happy with you when she hears the news."

Tammy packed her bags and took the Forty-Four bus to Penn Station. At ten o'clock that night, she called Mr. Foster from a payphone and told him her half of the story. After that she boarded a train home to South Jersey.

My feet and hands were trembling so bad when I got the call, Derrick had to take the phone and finish the conversation.

"What time did it happen?" Derrick asked. He shook his head and jotted down a few notes before he hung up. I looked up at him and said, "Call the airline and book a flight for the three of us, we can leave the jeep at the airport parking lot."

Derrick looked surprised at my sudden assertiveness and instant financial stability.

"Shanelle, we don't have that kind of money. Do you know how expensive that flight is going to be?"

I headed to the bedroom to pack a small bag for Troy and said, "I'll explain everything later, let's get home."

An all points bulletin was broadcasted over the police wire for Flaco's arrest. Little did anyone know, Flaco knew he wasn't going to get too far after he left my house, so he hid out in a tree and shrub filled lot parallel to the house until things cooled down. He peered over the bushes as police walked in and out of my house while the three of us caught a flight from Washington National Airport to Newark. During the flight, Derrick and I talked about the rumors and speculations surrounding Alex's murder and his possible connections with Garvey. He quietly watched me wolf down his meal and my meal without blinking twice. It was the first time anyone witnessed my stress and disorder combined into one lethal strategy. When I handed the tray to the flight attendant, Derrick patted my hand and stared into my eyes without uttering a word. When our flight landed, I called Candy from the airport. Clinton picked us up and drove us back to their house to get Troy settled. After that, we borrowed Clinton's car and she agreed to watch Troy while Derrick and I checked on the house.

When we pulled up in front of the house, an empty beer can graced the beginning of the walkway. I immediately sucked my teeth and kicked the can in frustration. Derrick picked it up and wrapped his arm around me as we headed inside. The stench of sweaty bodies and weed immediately engulfed my senses as I held my stomach. Derrick checked the basement and shut the door leading into the kitchen while he looked at my reaction.

"You don't want to go in there Shanelle. Maybe we can find a cleaning service to take care of the mess."

I shook my head and looked upstairs as my stomach began to sour. All I could think about was a quiet resolve in the bathroom. The stench of marijuana continued as I climbed each stair with thoughts of my past. I immediately ran to the bathroom with Derrick in hot pursuit. I closed the door behind me but he invaded my space and walked in while I forced my food up to the surface and into the toilet.

Derrick took a washcloth out the linen closet and soaked it under the stream of the bathtub faucet. His love for me and his bedside manner kicked in while I heaved up and down from instant relief.

"In times of stress this seems to be your comfort

zone Shanelle, but it's not good for you."

I stood at the sink and immediately washed my hands and gargled. My eyes turned in his direction. The realization suddenly hit me as I threw the empty cup to the ground.

"I haven't done this in a long time Derrick, there's nothing wrong with me!"

"There's no way out unless you get rid of this baggage and heal Shanelle, let me help you."

I shook my head in denial as my lips began to quiver.

"You can do it, I know you can."

Our eyes met in our confined space. Derrick wiped tears away from my anguished face and kissed my forehead.

"Let me get something to settle your stomach," Derrick softly replied. "There's a twenty-four hour pharmacy on Broad Street, I'll be back in forty minutes." Before he left, I gave him my set of keys to get back into the house.

By the time Derrick got in the car, I was laying on my bed resting with a cold compress on my head. Just outside, Flaco smiled as he watched Derrick pull off in Clinton's car. Opportunity became his friend as he suddenly remembered the keys he stole from the house. He held them up under the brightness of the moon and contemplated which of the three would give him access to his sick desire. This was his time of the early morning. His adrenaline was pumping at the maximum force of three men combined into one.

Under the cover of darkness, Flaco appeared from the brush and walked across the street with fast hurried steps. The first key he picked up slipped into the lock and immediately gained him entry into my house. His fists tightened at the side of his hips and relaxed again upon release. An unloaded glock sat in the waist band of his pants. Flaco placed one foot on the bottom of the stairs. My eyes immediately opened at the soft sound. Sitting up straight, I strained my ears and concluded that it was the sound of new creaks. The exhaust of a delivery truck heading down South Center Street buried the sound of eight steps as my eyes shifted back and forth. My fingers nervously tapped my thigh.

"Derrick? Derrick is that you?" I called.

There was no answer, but I knew someone was in the house.

"Tammy?" My body began to freeze.

The next voice heckled at my desperation and fear. In a high pitch voice, he mimicked, "Derrick, Tammy, is that you?"

Before I could act, he kicked the door open and stepped inside. His stench engulfed my nose while I backed up towards the wall and pleaded with him.

"What do you want?"

He laughed at my fearful plea.

"You, sweet ass," he replied.

Three steps brought him closer to the bed. I quickly pulled the lamp cord which revealed his face.

He put one hand on the bed and used the other to pull the gun out from behind his back.

"You prefer the lights on?"

"No!" I yelled, "Leave me alone!"

I watched his eyes shift to the light cord. The power in his fist and the weapon in his other hand forced my adrenaline into defense mode. Three hurried steps brought him within one foot of my reach. I looked down at the cord resting on my night stand. A sharpened pencil sat in my reach as he smiled at me. Before he yanked on the cord, in one swift motion, I grabbed the sharpened number two pencil and rammed it right into his eardrum. The slanted strike forced the pencil halfway down his ear as he screamed in horrific pain. He managed to knock me to the ground with a swift backhand across the face. That was easy to deal with. Steven and Mrs. Viv smacked me across the face to last me a lifetime. I jumped up and bolted for the door while he dropped to the floor in pain.

Derrick's forgetfulness forced him to turn around at South Harrison Street and Central Avenue. He left his wallet and didn't have any pocket money to make a purchase. He was also too conscientious to drive Clinton's car without a license. By the time he turned the corner of Crescent Avenue, I was barreling out the front door begging for help.

Derrick barely put the car in park when he saw me running down the street screaming. He immediately threw the car into park. I ran into his arms and gripped my nails into his back.

"He's in the house, he tried to rape me!"

Derrick pulled me away and began to run towards the front door. I couldn't catch him, but I managed to yell as my knees fell into the cold grass beneath me, "Derrick, please don't leave me!"

It was enough to make him stop in his tracks. All I could see was another man I loved dead in my arms from a bullet or a knife. As the commotion continued, the neighborhood watch took action.

"There's a woman screaming at 122 Crescent Avenue. Oh, no sir, no shots fired this time."

A squad car responded in less than five minutes while Flaco hid in the attic.

Derrick held me tight as I shouted to the officer, "He's still inside, upstairs!"

Backup units responded with the K-9 Unit in tow. Flaco managed to pull the pencil out of his ear, but the excruciating pain of his damaged eardrum humbled his surrender. A flashlight in his face forced his eyes into a squint.

"Flaco Santiago," the officer stated.

"Yeah," Flaco replied, as he held his throbbing ear.

"You are under arrest for the murders of Officer Alex Foster and Gigi Ramirez."

Flaco looked at the officer surprised. Two officers pulled him off the floor and began to read him his Miranda warnings.

The Truth

The next day, with Derrick by my side, we met with the local and federal task force to discuss Alex's murder. This time we met in Morristown with five new agents. We sat at an oval mahogany table. The view overlooked the downtown area. Derrick sat to my immediate right and held my hand under the table. I wondered what was racing through his mind as he heard the inside story.

I was assured that Alex was not a crooked cop and that he was secretly working with law enforcement to eradicate corruption among local and federal officers. During Alex's training in Philadelphia, the feds conducted satellite conferences with certain officers who were part of the inside sting. When the feds told Alex that I was at Garvey, they showed him all the evidence including Flaco's statements to Rico when I left. Derrick put his arm around me as my hand grasped my mouth at the thought of confronting Flaco twice in my lifetime under unthinkable circumstances. Listening to his voice on tape brought me back to the night he tried to assault me in East Orange. Derrick was the only person I told, so I was glad he was by my side to hear the news.

Alex's reaction to Flaco and Rico's conversation

brought out the worst in him. The feds said that Alex was
so irate, they had to pull him from the job because they
didn't think he could go undercover again without killing
Flaco. Since I was the only person in the room that knew
about Alex's unfortunate childhood, I pressed my lips
together without reaction. They were right, Alex would
have killed Flaco to protect my honor. Amazingly, he kept
his composure and remained a loyal officer. While I
continued to listen, the feds also said that Alex was sworn
to secrecy. He was forbidden to tell me the entire truth no
matter how difficult it was for him. Poor Alex, the secrets
he had to keep must have weighed so heavily on his heart,
he had no choice but to keep me like a caged butterfly.

 I looked at the agent and said, "How come Flaco
wasn't arrested after the operation?"

 The agent cleared his throat and said, "Honestly,
we didn't have anything on him. He was a messenger for
Rico, but most of his information had nothing to do with
the investigation." The agent folded his hands and said,
"In fact, that's why we were so surprised to hear that he
was bumped up to third in command when Rico was
arrested. When we started looking more closely at Flaco's
activities after the murder, we realized that Rico needed to
do something that wasn't obvious to any of us."

 "Killing my husband?" I asked.

 The agent nodded his head in agreement.

 "We also have strong reason to believe that Nick
knew about the hit and didn't warn us because when we
pulled Alex from the investigation after the Garvey
incident, Nick couldn't reach him by phone and assumed
Alex turned on him. In fact, your husband was working
with us the entire time."

 Still searching for answers, I asked, "What about
Jack?"

 The agent took a deep breath and said, "Jack and

Alex were loyal officers. Jack is doing some inside work for us right now but has to keep a low profile. He was instrumental in our case against Detective Nick Damiano."

While the agent continued to speak, I stopped him in mid sentence. "Wait, something doesn't sit right with me. If my husband was such a commendable officer, why was he such a wreck before the trial?"

The agent pressed his lips together and focused on his answer before he spoke.

"Mrs. Foster, we had a solid case against Rico including taped conversations, video surveillance..." He paused and said, "Well, you know all this, but Alex knew with certainty that he was going to have to testify about the bounty on your brother Steven. There was little he could do without blowing the investigation. The defense team in this case was prepared to make a mockery of your dignity by sensationalizing this case with the photos of you at Garvey. Frankly Mrs. Foster, he didn't want that to happen."

I looked into Derrick's eyes hoping that he could help me absorb the information. I put my hand on top of his and said, "I need to leave now."

The agent stood up and said, "One more thing Mrs. Foster..."

"Yes," I replied as I stood up.

"Along with Flaco's murder charges, we are going to add attempted rape and some other charges. We may use that as leverage to get him to testify against Rico, but we in no way want to diminish your rights as a victim of assault."

Derrick put his arm around me. Events from my past boiled to the surface, but closure for Alex was more important.

I held out my hand and said, "Do what you need to do, I will cooperate."

By the time we got back to Candy's house it was already three o'clock. Clinton and Candy listened to us tell our harrowing story while Derrick bounced Troy on his lap. I quickly excused myself and went upstairs to place a phone call to the Fosters. They were relieved to hear from me and surprised that the police made so much headway in Alex's murder. Mr. Foster put the phone on speaker mode so Mrs. Foster could speak to me. She was glad to hear the news and wept while she tried to contain herself.

"How's Troy Shanelle, we miss him so much."

"He's fine, he's downstairs, we're at Candy's house now."

"So what are your plans now?" Mr. Foster asked.

"Well, our flight leaves back to D.C. tomorrow night. I'll bring him to the house next weekend if you like." I would have let him stay for a week, but thoughts of Tammy didn't sit well with me.

Mrs. Foster exhaled into the phone, "That would be wonderful Shanelle," she replied.

Before I hung up the phone, I asked Mr. Foster to put 122 Crescent Avenue up for sale. He seemed relieved about that.

"Okay Shanelle, I'll take care of everything."

Derrick came upstairs to check on me. I hung up the phone while he knelt down on the floor. It was a well needed hug with small circles to my upper and lower back. When he looked up at me I said, "I'm fine, really."

"Really?" he asked.

"I'm ok, trust me, Dr. Derrick."

Derrick stroked my face and said, "I don't want to be a doctor in your eyes, just Derrick, okay?"

"Sure," I replied.

He cleared his throat and continued.

"If I were a zoo keeper, I would still want you to talk to someone Shanelle, you've been through a lot."

Troy could be heard in the distance laughing at Clinton. Thinking of him forced me to focus on the things that mattered.

I folded my hands on my lap and said, "I doubted Alex and I feel horrible about that. All he wanted was for me be safe and to be a good mother to our son."

Derrick silenced me by placing his finger to my lips.

"Shanelle, it's not like I'm trying to compete with Alex but I have to admit, after hearing what the feds had to say, he really loved you and did everything he could to protect his family. I'm sure he's looking down at you and thanking you for doing such a good job at raising little man. Don't be so hard on yourself, just hold on to the things that matter."

He didn't need to say anything else, I knew he was right.

"I'll look up someone in D.C., I promise."

Derrick pulled me off the bed and said, "Good, that's what I wanted to hear."

We got back to D.C. without fail, but I remembered feeling extremely numb inside and out. I called in sick the next day and sat around with Derrick and Troy like a mummy. Derrick knew I was feeling the emotional brunt of my ordeal. He left a book on the kitchen table. The chapter heading read "Post Traumatic Stress Disorders." I wondered if he was sizing me up mentally. Honestly, I didn't know where to start or end, but it was time to pick up the phone and talk to somebody. By that evening, we found a therapist in the area who was willing to meet me.

I reassured Derrick that I was going to meet with her, but I had strong reservations. I kept so many secrets to myself, I wondered if I could open up to a complete stranger. By nightfall, my mind was made up, I didn't want to go.

"Derrick, just give me a chance. I'm not backing out, I just need to figure out that part of my life that seems so empty."

Derrick was concerned, but forgiving.

"Look, if it doesn't feel right after I try it my way, then I'll go."

Derrick voiced his own perception.

"You know Shanelle, just because Steven had a few things rolling around in his head, doesn't mean you're crazy. I just want you to feel like the decisions you make aren't based on stress or anxiety. I never told you this, but I felt like that was the reason you married Alex. But don't get me wrong, it's also the reason I told you it was your turn."

The revelation sent chills through my body, but he was right. The only thing I needed to do was put the pieces together without help from anyone. My father's revelation left a huge gap in my life and I was craving a biological connection with someone. With earnest, I began to think about the things my father told me after Alex's funeral.

"Her name was Clara," I said to Derrick. His face was full of compassion.

"I'm so sorry Shanelle," He said.

I laid on his chest and began to contemplate my needs.

"When we get back to Jersey, I'm going to my father's old job to see if anyone remembers her."

Derrick ran his fingers through my hair and said, "That sounds like a good idea."

"What about you Derrick," I asked. "Do you ever wonder about your father?"

Derrick pressed his forehead up against mine and said, "Yeah, but I buried it Shanelle. Besides, it would hurt my mother if I did and I couldn't do that to her." Knowing Derrick the way I did, it was safe to take the "manly" way out and avoid his issues.

"Do you feel connected?" I asked.

Derrick sighed and said, "Honestly I do. I know I won't make the same mistakes my father did." He paused as he looked for rationale in his answer.

"I look at Troy and even though he's not my son, I want to do the right thing and be there for him."

It was the first time I heard Derrick talk about a real commitment to Troy.

"What should we do about that, I haven't thought about it because everything just fell into place for us."

Derrick grabbed my face and said, "I want you by my side Shanelle. I told you before, once I start my residency, I'm going to be working around the clock, but I want to come home to you."

I pulled the sheet up to my neck and said, "Well, I'll have my degree by the end of the summer session. In September I'll start my masters program."

Derrick leaned on his elbow and said, "Well, we'll be busy getting in debt together I guess."

I laughed at first because debt wasn't an issue for me at all, but I wasn't ready to share that information with Derrick until I had a better idea where our relationship was going.

"Well, I told Mr. Foster to put the house up for sale. I don't want to go back there. Whatever money I make on the proceeds can help pay for my expenses."

Derrick pulled me into his frame and said, "I'm going to camp out at my mother's house until I can find an apartment. I think we should do this the right way."

"What do you mean the right way?" I asked.

Derrick sucked his teeth and said, "Shanelle, don't play with me. We're shackin' up now, but I did it because it was last minute. When we get home, I need to make a respectable woman out of you my sugar shack girl."

I started laughing and said, "We'll see. In the mean time, I'm going to enroll Troy in preschool three days a week."

Derrick stroked his eyebrows and said, "Good, he's more than ready, Lord knows he gets all of our attention."

I agreed by quietly replying, "He's a lucky little boy."

Derrick wrapped his arms around me and said, "I'm a lucky man Shanelle."

"I'm just as lucky as you are Derrick."

He stared into my eyes and said, "I hope you can close some chapters in your life now."

"I will," I replied, "As soon as I find out some information about my real mother."

Loose Ends

My internship in Washington wrapped up in three weeks with a few contacts and a solid A plus on my research paper. In that short period of time, Mr. Foster arranged for a mover to pack up the house and placed everything in storage down in South Jersey. The house was sold in three months to an out of state couple. Needless to say, the neighbors were glad to see the last member of the Brown family leave the neighborhood.

Derrick and I scoured the newspapers for weeks to find two decent apartments that were reasonably close in location. After an exhaustive search, we ended up finding a real estate agent who found a two family house in Montclair with two vacant apartments. The arrangement was perfect for the two of us because it allowed us to have our space and be close to each other. Troy loved the arrangement too because a common access door allowed him to go up and down the stairs between the two of us without a fuss.

By mid September, we settled into our planned routines. Derrick was six weeks into his exhaustive residency at University Hospital, Troy started preschool and I started my masters program at St. James University. To keep the Fosters happy, we agreed that Troy would spend every other weekend with them, including

Mondays. Mr. Foster drove him back on Monday afternoons and Derrick was usually there to greet him at the door. Each time Mr. Foster brought Troy home, they spent hours talking and grunting about sports, the trial, politics and life in general. It was Derrick's only day off, but I think he looked forward to the time he spent with Mr. Foster and Troy. I knew Mr. Foster cherished their talks because he was filling the void of his cherished son.

On a cool sunny day in November, I walked in the house and found the two of them standing in the lobby shaking hands and laughing.

"Hey Shanelle," Mr. Foster said, "I was just leaving."

"Well, look at the two of you, what are you so happy about?"

They both responded in unison, "Nothing!"

The look on their faces was suspicious, but Troy distracted me.

"Look mommy, I found two worms!"

I pretended to be happy to have his happy discovery on my living room floor.

"That's nice, but take it outside."

Mr. Foster patted Derrick on the back and gave me a hug. "Listen, let me get on the road, I'll give you a call later." He suddenly remembered something with a snap to his fingers. "Oh yeah, mom wants all of you over for Thanksgiving, can you come?"

I looked at Derrick and immediately thought about how we were going to work it all out. Derrick immediately cured my doubt.

"Well, I have an early shift, but if my mother can come with us, we would love to come."

Mr. Foster smiled and said, "Hey, that sounds like a plan."

"Great!" I replied, "Maybe your mother can stay

the weekend at my house. We can walk on the beach, Troy really misses that."

Derrick winked and said, "Well, I won't be able to stay but that could work."

We said our goodbyes at the end of the walkway while Derrick hid a secret from me. It was written all over his face, but he wouldn't tell me.

"What?" I asked. "You're keeping something from me."

"Nothing," he replied. Then he picked up his football off the front lawn and said, "Troy, long pass!"

Troy ran down to the other side and caught the ball. He fell backwards, but immediately threw the ball down.

"Touch down!" he yelled as he clapped his hands. Derrick put his arm around me and said, "Like I said, nothing."

While Derrick opted to keep his secret to himself, I walked into the kitchen to unearth another one.

"Yes please, New York City, may I have the number to the Emory Roth Group?"

I scribbled the number down and sat down at the table. Derrick washed his hands and handed Troy a paper towel to dry his hands off.

"Hi, good afternoon, can you connect me to human resources, I'm trying to obtain information on an employee who used to work there."

Elevator music followed. I looked up at Derrick. He gave me a thumbs up and ushered Troy back outside with two apples in tow.

"Hi, is this human resources?"

"Yes it is how can I help you?"

"Um, well, my name is Shanelle Brown, my father William Brown…"

"Yes, Shanelle, how are you, this is Betty Roberts,

I remember your father."

"Oh great," I replied. "Well, I was wondering if you could help me find out some information about my mother Clara…"

"Excuse me?" Betty asked, she seemed startled, but continued, "Clara died in a car accident years ago, if this is some kind of a joke…"

"I'm sorry," I replied. "But to be honest with you, my father told me that they had an affair and when she died, my father took custody of me…"

Betty began to muffle the phone and I couldn't hear the commotion. She began to breathe heavily into the phone before she spoke.

"Shanelle, I have to ask, how old are you?"

"Twenty-three."

Betty immediately gasped. "I can't believe this. Can you come to the office today? We have a box of her belongings in the archive office, but no one claimed it. I think she has a sister in Virginia, but we couldn't reach her."

My heart started to beat in rapid succession.

"Can I have your address?" I asked. I quickly jotted the number down as Derrick walked back into the house with Troy.

"Is everything okay Shanelle?" Derrick asked.

"Everything is fine, there's information on my mother at the office."

Derrick's eyes widened when I told him.

"Do you want us to go with you?" He asked.

"No, keep Troy, I know you're tired. Can you manage?"

Derrick kissed me on my lips. A tap on my thigh followed. I looked down at my growing pride and joy and said, "Yes?"

"Can I have a kiss too mommy?" Troy asked.

"How about three?" I replied.

Troy giggled and held his face out while I pecked him three times.

Derrick walked me to the door and wished me good luck as I headed into the city.

By the time I reached West 35th Street in Manhattan, I got so nervous I had to pull over and catch my breath. I placed my forehead on the steering wheel and talked myself into bringing closure to my life. I jumped back into traffic and searched for a parking space. A tiny elevator took me to the eleventh floor of the Emory Roth Group. The reaction of the woman at the reception desk was a sign that she had been there for more than twenty-three years.

When I reached the desk, she stood up with a dropped jaw. She kept her composure and said, "You must be Shanelle, Betty is expecting you."

"Thank you," I replied.

The woman walked around the desk and put her hand on my shoulder. "I've been with this firm for thirty years and I knew your mother. It's amazing how much you look like Clara."

An elevator door opened. A woman with slim hips stepped off and immediately gasped when she saw me. The receptionist reacted to Betty's surprised look on her face. Betty grabbed my hand and said, "I can't believe it, you look just like your mother."

Tears began to well up in my eyes as I looked at the two of them.

"Please, can you tell me about her, do you have a picture?"

We stepped on the elevator together and immediately began to probe each other with questions.

"So what are you doing now Shanelle, and how is your father?"

"I'm in school, he's fine I guess, what did my mother do here?"

"Oh," Betty replied. "She did a little bit of everything, public relations, marketing, she was phenomenal."

"Really, I can't wait to see a picture of her."

Betty led me to a small copy office and reached up to retrieve a dusty box off the top shelf. It was marked, *"Clara R. Johnson."*

"Johnson?" I asked. "That was her last name?"

Betty said, "Yes, that's right."

"Oh," I rolled my eyes in my head and thought, *"With my luck, Derrick is probably my long lost cousin."*

Betty eased my worry and said, "There are so many people with that name though, it's common. I do know that Clara had a sister in Fairfax, Virginia, but they had a strained relationship while she was here."

"Oh," I replied. "You sure do know a lot about my mother, were you close?"

Betty laughed out loud and said, "You might say that."

"Is there somewhere I can sit?" I asked.
Betty smiled and said, "Take your time, the only thing I need you to do is fill out a claim form for the contents in the box."

"Sure," I replied.

Instead of sitting on a chair, I plopped down on the floor and took the lid off the box. I immediately inhaled at the sight of a three by five inch picture of my mother. She was standing up with her hands on her hips smiling wider than I ever smiled in my entire life. I stroked the picture with complete joy in my eyes and bellowed out, "Hi mama, it's me Shanelle."

I quickly looked around to see if anyone heard me. My pointer finger stroked the entire frame of her body on the photograph. She had thick thighs and a big forehead just like me and Troy. I began to laugh as Alex's references to Sade's head came to mind. More photographs followed along with happy tears. She had wild wooly hair like I did and I wondered if she ever used Nunile.

At the bottom of the box, there were little messages and love notes to my father. On one she wrote:

To W.B.

How quaint are we.
The sweetest apricots,
Satin sheets and forget me nots,
Suddenly love makes three.

A love untold,
Beauty behold,
Our love child wrapped in white gold.

Sadly our gem cannot shine,
Your love will never be mine
We have yet to be defined.
Except for the garnet ring I wear...
so surreal and consciously sublime.

This life belongs to us.
Forever yours in the eyes of our love child...
Clara

I held the poem to my heart and began to cry. My whimsical need to write poetry came from mother. The precious ring my father gave to my mother was passed down to me to protect my virtuosity. I cried harder because I cursed my father out when he asked me about the wherabouts of my garnet gem. Knowing that it was my mother's ring brought more tears of joy to my eyes as I wiped my hands on my jeans just to gain composure. I couldn't wait to share the news with Derrick, so I placed everything back in the box and headed back to Betty's office. By the time I reached her, she could see the relief in my eyes.

I gave her a hug and filled out the forms. She gave her coworker a pocket camera and took a picture of my happiness.

"Good luck Shanelle, I'm glad we didn't get rid of the box."

I smiled back as I got on the elevator and waved goodbye. I felt like the luckiest girl in the world.

Derrick met me at the door with Troy and Candy's big ass belly. She was ready to pop, but she couldn't wait to see my treasure.

Derrick chatted with us for an hour and then retired for the night with a warm kiss to my forehead. He was as shocked as I was about my mother's resemblance. Troy gave him a high five and said, "Now go to bed Dr. Dee!" Derrick laughed and said, "Shanelle, when you get a chance, can you pull my car in the driveway so I won't get a ticket."

Candy and I were laughing, but I managed to respond, "Okay, I will, goodnight." I fed Troy his dinner and sent him to bed without a major fuss. He was already worn out from the long trip up from South Jersey. Candy and I continued to scour over every ounce of my mother's life while I rejoiced in her beautiful spirit. Candy said of her, "She seemed like she was real down to earth and fun to be with, just like you girl." I kissed Candy on the cheek and said, "Thank you little mama."

She rubbed her belly and said, "Girl one more week, I can't wait until the princess gets here." She stood up to leave while I picked up her pocket book.

"Did you figure out a name yet?"

"Bianca Noel," Candy replied.

"Cute," I said, "I like that."

She turned to leave and said, "Don't forget to move the good doctor's car."

I grabbed his jacket and put it on while we headed for the door. When I walked outside, the car was already parked. I waved goodbye to Candy and thought, "Derrick must be going crazy, he already parked the car." I reached into his jacket pocket to hang his car keys on the hook by the exit, but there were no keys. Instead, my hands felt a small velvet box. I took it out of his pocket and stared. I laughed at first because I knew Derrick was a pure clown and I didn't know what he was up to. I checked on Troy and quietly walked upstairs. I turned the door knob but it was locked. We never locked the inside doors because it was easier for Troy to get to us.

"Derrick?" I called.

He didn't answer. Three knocks followed.

"Who is it?" He asked in a burly voice.

"Stop playing Derrick, open the door," I said.

"What's the password?" he asked. I could tell by the brevity in his voice that he was smiling.

"We don't have passwords silly."

"Did you park my car?" he asked.

"You parked it, open the door."

"Shanelle," he whispered.

"Yes," I replied.

The door quickly opened.

"You finally said the password," Derrick said.

"I did?" I asked.

Derrick took the small velvet box out of my hand and said, "Did you open it?"

I shook my head no and said, "You open it, it's

probably a Hershey kiss, you practical joker."

Derrick laughed and as corny as he was, he got down on his knees and said, "I may not have much to give you now, but I need to walk this earth with you by my side Shanelle. I want to be a father to Troy. I can't replace his father, but I think I'm doing a good job."

Derrick grabbed my waist and kissed my stomach with a soft peck. He looked up at me and said, "I'll support any dream or aspiration you have in this lifetime baby. You're the only one that did that for me, just say yes Shanelle." Derrick took the ring out of the sleeve and slipped a petite emerald cut ring on my finger.

"You can have anything in the world you want, just say yes."

Derrick stood up to kiss me with a smile on his face. Before he kissed me he said, "I was praying that you came home with some good news. I didn't want any more heartache to come your way about your family. I told myself when you left that if you heard one more negative thing, Troy and I would be enough family for a lifetime."

A lifetime indeed. That night we organized our lives for the future. A four year engagement, discreet nights of privacy when Troy was home and buck wild sex while he stayed with the Fosters during long weekends.

Truth be told, I needed to let Derrick know that I was financially stable. Before I did, I went to the bank and obtained a cashier's check for One Hundred and Forty-five Thousand dollars. It was Derrick's loan balance from medical school. I remembered when Alex paid for my first year at Bloomberg College. He said he did it because it would only help us in the long run. He was right. Even though he was gone, my life with Derrick and Troy was a good thing and I knew Alex would be happy for me. The money wasn't an issue anyway. With him or without him, I knew I could make it on my own.

Family Affair

The feds and the prosecutors didn't let me down. An intense investigation brought Flaco to his knees in one double murder trial. He served Rico to them on a platter with his knees knocking together in pure fear. Redemption came to him in prison. There was little remorse from either of them as we sat in a packed courtroom to hear the sentence. Tammy cleaned up her act and sat quietly next to her father as she wept her guilt away. I sat next to Derrick and held his hand with pride and sadness. In my other hand was a trifold locket Candy gave me after Bianca was born. There were three delicate pictures resting inside each frame. One of myself, Troy and the other was a refurbished picture of my mother. It was a sweet gesture from my best friend in the whole world. The locket was enhanced by my garnet ring. This time it was a source of maternal strength and emotional closure.

Every now and then, Mrs. Foster peeked at me and Derrick. The last time she looked at me she smiled and nodded her head in approval as she stared at my hand resting in Derrick's smooth grip. It was a gentle understanding despite it all.

Four years couldn't come quick enough for us to get married. With the Foster's blessings, Derrick adopted

Troy six months before his fifth birthday. He told everyone he knew that his "police officer daddy," was in heaven and his other daddy was a doctor. With Derrick's help, we made a scrap book for Troy so he could carry it around whenever he wanted. He was so proud of his two fathers, he took the book with him to school for his first day of kindergarten.

The following year, Derrick finished his residency and took his medical boards. Without fail, he passed with flying colors. He opened a flourishing pediatrics practice in Newark and worked day and night until he figured out a comfortable pace. As busy as he was, if Troy called he stopped everything to talk to his son. It didn't matter if it was a simple spelling word, Troy had his ear. I gave Derrick plenty of space when it came to the two of us. There was so much intensity in him to become a competent doctor, I made sure that his office ran smooth by hiring two assistants and an office manager. At a minimum, the only rigors of his practice were the rise and fall of abused and neglected children.

Derrick's toughest case came to him when a distraught woman came in with her daughter. She was barely conscious when she brought the frail child in for treatment. Burns and three week old bruises covered her body from head to toe. Derrick was furious when he questioned her mother and signaled the nurse to contact Child Protective Services and an ambulance.

Derrick was startled when he opened the limp child's eyes to check her pupils. She had the most beautiful green eyes he had ever seen. He couldn't believe that anyone could be so cruel to a child. Derrick saw abuse before, but this case was different. Her mother, Cora Mae slipped out the back door and went back to her abandoned apartment. Fearing an immediate arrest for the harm she caused her daughter, she held her hands steady and slipped a noose around her neck. The strain of caring for a child born from rape was too much for her drug addicted soul. Her feet swayed back and forth as the police banged on the door. While her mother rocked back and forth under the force of the rope, Derrick finally convinced the little girl to recite her name.

"Corinthia," she replied with a soft whimper.

When Derrick came home, he took a long shower. The reality of his uncomplicated domestic world and the social plagues that walked into his office forced him to smother me with hugs and kisses under a thick comforter.

I took off my glasses and said, "What's wrong?" Derrick rubbed his eyes and placed his head in my lap.

"It gets crazy sometimes Shanelle. After four years of an intense residency, you think you've seen it all and then you get knocked for a loop again."

I stroked the fine lines in Derrick's brow. His skin was still smooth as satin as I kissed his forehead with caring confidence.

"Perspectives change when you look through the eyes of a child," Derrick said. "I can't imagine what that little girl must have gone through, she's only eight years old." His strain drifted off as his eyes closed. I held his hand and kissed it with a soft peck. The stress in our lives stemmed from the social and medical needs of others, but Derrick knew when and how to turn it off. He turned his face into my stomach and stroked my collarbone with the tips of his fingers.

"I'm taking Thursday and Friday off so we can have a long weekend. Let's go to the shore home, I need to get away."

"Sure," I replied.

That weekend we went to the beach. I rested on Derrick's chest with confidence as he read his New England Journal of Medicine. I was accustomed to his dual track mind while he stroked my hair and absorbed himself in medicine and science. Troy appeared as a silhouette in the same way his father did so long ago. He had Alex's broad shoulders supported by strong legs that were growing thick and firm as the days went by. Troy got up and walked over to me and Derrick. He picked up his football and said, "Dad do you wanna play football?"

Derrick put his journal down and said, "Sure, go out for a long pass."

I chuckled to myself as Derrick looked back and smiled. *"If he only knew,"* I thought.

Fun and frolic brought us home early that night. There was no need to don pretty panties or a cute bra for Derrick. As soon as Troy went to sleep, we made love without the song and dance of foreplay. Our skin intertwined under the sheets as Derrick locked his hands into mine and made love to me under the brightest orange moon. I don't remember the last time seeing such a beautiful twilight and feeling so free.

Two years later, that same twilight graced an outside wedding on the beach as close friends and relatives held up a glass in our honor. Bianca chased Troy in her lily white flower girl dress while he entertained his bratty little godsister by ducking and dodging her in the deep sand. Derrick's mother couldn't stop crying and neither could Mrs. Foster. The strangest family bonds formed and biology didn't matter.

I walked out to the shoreline with Derrick and stared at the moon. I quietly said hello to Alex with a whisper. His love kept me safe, Derrick's love made me whole. I bent down in my dress and drew a heart for the two of them as the water rushed in and quickly erased it away. Derrick slipped his hand around my waist and escorted me away from the seemingly quiet shoreline. Life never felt so good to me when I was with him or alone writing poetry.

Three years of family life quickly passed us by while we watched Troy grow before our eyes. The idea of motherhood swelled in my head day and night while Derrick passionately entertained my biological clock. On a warm September day, Derrick, with the help of a midwife, helped me bring into the world a seven pound one ounce baby girl. She was the little princess of the house and in Derrick and Troy's eyes, I was still the queen. We spent endless days at the beach house and put an extension on the back to accommodate our growing family. Raising a family and working part time as a freelance writer became my resolve. I also dusted off Alex's old camera and took up photography. It was all the therapy I needed with the life I left behind. Every time we spent time at the beach house, the ocean became my reflection in the warmth of Derrick's embrace. Life for me was empowering, simple, sexy and sweet.

THE END

Moody's Soapbox

Well, you haven't read the last from me, I'm probably writing as you read this message. I would love to hear from you, especially by email. Send me your opinions, reviews, hopes and dreams. I'll be waiting...

Moody@moodyholiday.com

I don't want to leave you hanging for my next project, so take a moment to read a "snip it" from Portia's tasty tale.

Portia's Little Black Book

By Moody Holiday

www.moodyholiday.com

"Malik"

973.555.2222

Portia woke up to a blustery wind just outside her bedroom window. She took a deep breath and rolled over for another round of sleep. As soon as she nestled into a comfortable position, her cell phone began to vibrate on the nightstand. By the third ring, the pulsating charge forced the phone to the edge. She usually knocked it to the floor in annoyance, but this call required special attention. Portia announced herself with a soft voice as a hollow noise filled the earpiece.

"Hello."

Brief static followed.

"Hello," she stated.

"Portia," he said, "Can you hear me?" Malik's voice was thick and deep, glazed over with warm cream. Static came in and out of the phone again as Portia looked at the clock. "Where are you?" she asked.

"Just outside of Philly. Pick me up at terminal C by two thirty." He meant business when he said it, even though he needed forgiveness. Malik was hard to please at times, but he always meant well despite his commanding ways.

Portia sensed the need in his voice and began to relax. She sighed and immediately spread her legs under the comforter.

Malik sensed something unusual and said, "What's wrong?"

Her answer was quick and wrought with denial. "Flight Thirty-three right?"

Malik sighed out loud and threw his Black Enterprise Magazine in the empty first class seat next to him. He leaned forward and placed his weary head in his hands. The base in his voice beckoned Malik's need for her. "I'm sorry baby."

Portia closed her thighs and applied pressure to Kitty as she began to massage her.

Slight turbulence broke Malik's concentration as he looked out the passenger window and then came into focus again. With one massive hand, he stroked his goatee and reclined back into his seat. All he could think about was finding a way to slow things down with her.

"Let's stay in bed today," Malik said.

"I'm there," Portia softly replied, as her breasts began to ache at the sound of his voice.

Malik closed his eyes and immediately became aroused by her response. Then he asked an important question.

"Do you have my key?"

Portia was so wrapped up in the small tremors between her legs, she began to lose focus.

"What?" She asked in return.

"Do you have my key?" Malik replied.

Portia refused to answer his inquiry. The question turned her off as she pulled her hand out of Kitty's den and rested it at her side.

Before she closed the phone shut she replied, "Two thirty Malik."

Malik calmly slipped his phone in his dress shirt. He began to smile and stroked each side of his face with his powerful hands. As the plane began to descend to a lower altitude, Malik relaxed and thought about his girl wonder.

The last time they were together, Malik took Portia on vacation to Belize. It was just what their relationship needed. The only set back was Malik's career. As a United States Federal Marshall, "duty calls," came first.

On the first day, Malik treated Portia to a full day of snorkeling off of Hamanasi's Barrier reef. Portia donned a coral blue bikini to enhance her skin color. By days end, the sun glazed her over in satin crimson like a lost survivor on a stranded island.

Malik pulled out all the stops and rented the best diving gear money could buy. He also paid a hotel servant one hundred dollars to prepare a picnic basket filled with fresh fruit, lobsters, goat cheese and chocolate. The only thing Portia needed to do was be a lady by day and a freak by night fall.

By the time the sun laid to rest, Malik escorted Portia to a cab and packed the trunk with purchases from the local island shops. Portia slid over to the far right of the cab so Malik could lay his head in her lap. During the quiet ride back to their cabana, Portia stroked Malik's hair line with the tips of her fingers while he serenaded her. If Larry Graham ever had a twin vocalist for a brother, Malik was the one. Portia stared into his eyes while he stroked her delicate neckline and ran his finger into her oiled over cleavage.

When they reached the cabana, a full day of sand, sweat and sweet island drinks clogged their pores. Malik picked her up and threw her over his massive shoulder while Portia relaxed like a succulent rag doll. Thoughts of Malik inside of her caused goose bumps to rise and fall on her arm. Neither one of them wanted to shower. Malik craved the sweet and pungent remains of the day and

Portia preferred salt in various places.

That night Portia treated his rock hard muscles *to* a full body message on a king size. She straddled his waist and put her hair in a neat ponytail. Malik tried to reach for one of her nipples, but she made him put his hand back down.

"Be still," she whispered.

As Malik continued to reminisce, the captain announced his descent into Newark. The beast in Malik's pants became aroused and pulsated in different directions as he used his hand to calm himself down. His moment with Portia continued.

"What if I don't?" he asked.

Portia immediately reached around and grabbed his lifeline. In a quick defensive reaction, Malik grabbed her by the shoulders and pulled her on top of him. Portia started laughing as she looked into his dreamy light brown eyes. Malik wrapped his arm around her and slid his hand down her back. He used his hand to spread her butt apart until he reached her creamy middle. Portia moaned and opened her legs for easier access. In an instant, the beast stood up while Portia took a bow right on top of him. Her face mellowed down and relaxed as she reached behind and massaged his silky accoutrements. Despite three hours of under water exploration, Portia rocked Malik into an easy state of mind for twenty fun filled minutes.

The rumbling vibration of the plane's touch down into Newark Airport enhanced her spectacular finish as Malik stretched his brawny arms into the air and then shivered from his brief recollection.

Malik stepped into the aisle and cocked his head to the left and then to the right. His gun holster needed a quick adjustment as the courteous flight attendant handed Malik his travel bag. Before he exited, Malik knocked on the cock pit door and waited for a response. His frat brother opened the door and immediately gave him dap.

"Smooth flight," Malik said, as Clinton pushed down various control switches.

"Anytime man, thanks for the security."

Malik lowered his head and stepped onto the jet way anxiously awaiting the sight of Portia. When he reached the end, she was no where to be found. The only thing waiting for him was a slim man in a black suit holding his name on a piece of white cardboard. Malik sighed and greeted the driver as they headed to the taxi and bus lanes.

In the time it took Portia to make arrangements for Malik, a few family matters popped up.

Portia's father knocked on her bedroom door when she finished her call with Malik.

"Portia," he commanded. "Help me with your mother, I'll be gone most of the day."

Portia rolled her eyes in her head and threw back her comforter. She followed her father into her parent's master bedroom as her mother laid in bed listless and lethargic.

A syringe, cotton balls and two needles were neatly lined on her nightstand with a day old glass of water. Portia walked into her parent's private bathroom and quickly washed her hands. She walked back into the bedroom and plopped on their bed. A temporary gaze was shared between them as Portia tucked strands of hair behind her mother's ear. The despondent look in her eye was consistent with drug enhanced sobriety.

Portia's father stood at the edge of the bed as Portia quickly put on a pair of latex gloves. Her father's serious expression and demonstrative stance ensured that Portia did it right the first time.

"Tie it once, then run your finger along her vein."

"I know, I know," Portia said.

"Good," he replied. "You're on your own tomorrow, so make sure you get it right." He crossed his arms against his chest as Portia slid the needle into her mother's vein for instant relief. Sylvia smiled as her porcelain doll frame became warm on the inside. On the outside, she looked like the next episode of the bedtime crypt keeper.

Heavy footsteps exited the room. Her father's departure was nothing more than domestic abandonment. Portia waited until he was out of earshot and said, "I'll bring you a tray before I leave mother."

Sylvia gathered the strength to reply, "Oh please, I'd like English tea sandwiches, no crust."

A delicate kiss tapped her mother's forehead as Portia got up to leave. "Of course mother, nothing but the best."

Portia's command of culinary style and elegance came from countless summers at an expensive cooking school in Rhode Island. No matter the dish, Portia could slam. She washed her hands again and went downstairs to prepare a feast for Malik and a dieter's plate for her delicate drunken mother. Portia intended to even the score with Malik for leaving her behind in Belize, but parts of her genuinely ached for him as she thought about his massive hands roving up her thighs.

By the time she reached his apartment in Palisades Park, the only thing left to do was to let the cleaning lady in while she finished setting the table. Portia threw his extra key in a glass bowl and beckoned Mary to hurry the job.

"Make sure you clean the bathroom twice, I want it spotless," Portia said. She lit two candles and quickly covered choice select salmon with marinated portabella mushrooms. Fifteen minutes before his arrival, she pushed Mary out the door and unbuttoned her blouse. She smelled her hands and immediately rubbed a cut lemon on them to reduce the smell of seasonings on her skin. Portia looked in the mirror and slicked her hair back with a light moisturizer. She took a quick shower and while inside, prepped Kitty with cocoa butter oil for Malik's arrival.

Malik opened the door and immediately dropped his bags in the foyer. His smile was instant and self assured. The sound of a shower and an immaculate condo were sure fired ways to tug at his hard heart. Malik washed his hands and patted them against a kitchen towel. He immediately sampled buttery crackers prepared with cream cheese and sun dried tomatoes. He took a deep breath as he savored the taste and cleaned his teeth with his tongue.

Steam began to escape from the shower down the hall. The warm condensed air tapped his neck as he turned around to find Portia wrapped in a towel.

"Hey baby," he said, with a caring smile. "Still mad?"

Portia tried to walk past him to tease his senses but it didn't work. He pulled the towel off of her and threw it to the floor. In one fell swoop, Malik picked her up off the floor. Half of Portia's body dangled upside down as Malik carried her into the bedroom with three hard core spanks to her butt that left a pretty purple bruise.

Malik threw her on the bed and brushed his goatee against her nipples. His soft facial hair enticed her back to arch and call his name. In small delicate circles, Malik used his thumb and explored her swollen region. With three soft bites, he marked her body in three places to last four weeks before his next transport.

Malik slowly buried his face between her legs. Moans mixed with, "I missed you," whispered from Portia's anxious breath, as Malik's long tongue tasted her creamy buttermilk.

Portia squeezed her legs together and locked his head there while intensity built up inside of her. She held his hand in quiet commitment. They never said, "I love you," but he knew he was the only man to enjoy such pleasure.

Malik stuck his tongue inside of her and squeezed her thighs with intense pressure. He wanted to make it right since he left her hanging in Belize…

Feelin' Moody?

www.moodyholiday.com